Also by John F. Rooney

Nine Lives Too Many
The Daemon in Our Dreams
The Rice Queen Spy
Clawed Back from the Dead
Last Passage to Santiago

UNPROTECTED LOVE

a novel by

John F. Rooney

Senneff House Publishers
Fort Lauderdale, Florida

Senneff House Publishers
P.O. Box 11601
Fort Lauderdale, FL 33339
www.senneffhouse.com

This book is a work of fiction. Names, characters, places, and incidents either are products of the author's imagination or are used fictitiously. Any resemblance to actual events or locales or persons, living or dead, is entirely coincidental.

Copyright © 2011 by John F. Rooney

All rights reserved,
including the right of reproduction
in whole or in part in any form.

Cover design by Kevin Stawieray
Inside book design and formatting by Dawn Von Strolley Grove
Cover illustratiion by Brian Collins

Manufactured in the United States of America

ISBN-13: 978-0-9752756-1-0
ISBN-10: 0-9752756-1-5

For
Leonard W. Rooney, Jr.
1925-2010

1

Under the raw, unforgiving floodlights, the lifeless blue eyes of the murdered boy stared up at the starless sky. As Denny studied the victim—blond, fair-skinned and handsome—he felt an enormous sadness along with a sense of futility and despair about a world where such things were permitted to happen. He stared down for more than a minute at the body lying on the rotting timbers of the pier, taking in the grisly sight as two personas, one a fellow human being viewing gaping death, and the other that of a professional cop trying to piece together evidence and process essential information.

When Denny stepped back, he almost slipped and had to be caught by Sergeant Rich Walters, a member of his special ops task force. Rich said, "Whoa, Den. Watch yourself. It's slippery out here."

Denny steadied himself on a piling.

Rich said, "This is the third kid they've found in the last three months—all young guys—all dropped somewhere along the waterfront."

Denny asked, "Any ID on this one?"

His question was answered by the third member of the squad, Teresa Kerrigan. The three of them first began working together in the NYPD Grand Central detail set up after Nine-Eleven. "Nothing. Pockets empty. No jewelry. No personal stuff."

Terry looked like she'd dressed in a hurry. She'd thrown on a Hofstra University sweatshirt, white Nikes, a Red Sox cap, and a pair of worn jeans. The two men were wearing blue windbreakers with NYPD in large white letters emblazoned on the back of the jackets.

Denny said, "Look at the boy's mouth. Doesn't it seem to be bulging? I'm going to see if there's something in there."

Denny wondered why he called him a boy, but he did look young and vulnerable. Denny stretched on his latex gloves and leaned over. He hated to touch the dead body, any dead body. He pried open the mouth and probed inside. Under the lips, he dislodged something.

Denny said, "Christ, it's a condom in a wrapper."

Rich held out an open evidence bag, and Denny dropped the condom wrapped in blue plastic into the bag.

Denny said, "What about the other two cases? Is this a pattern, a signature or something?"

Terry answered, "I haven't followed the other two cases. It was only when Hal Madden of Central Homicide reminded us of the other two cases that we thought there might be a connection. We'll have to check the files of the two previous homicides."

Denny knelt next to the body and dictated comments into his tiny tape recorder: "Check condition of kid's teeth. See if well cared for. Body has neck abrasions and bruises. Wearing an Abercrombie tee shirt, Calvin jeans, Reeboks, no socks, looks to be in late teens, perhaps early twenties, thin. Body faceup. Looks like someone arranged this crime scene, staged it. He's laid out like a corpse in a casket with hands folded primly over chest, feet together, as if in respect for the dead, as if this were a family member—perhaps someone known, not a stranger."

He shut off the recorder and turned to the others. "Any other pertinent details?"

Before they could answer, everyone turned. Denny swiveled around and saw a uniformed officer, shining his flashlight down, leading someone, a person who was making a racket, out on the pier. As the figure approached, Denny realized it was Dr. Otis Lanning, an associate medical examiner, an old friend of Denny's and of his father. He was way beyond retirement age. A curmudgeon, but a sharp and knowledgeable doctor.

"Well, look who we have here. Dennis Tracy. New York's most famous dickhead. How she hanging? Den, how's Pops? Doing okay? Still in Florida, is he?"

Denny took the offered gnarled hand and shook it firmly. Lanning had huge wattles under his chin. His skin was gray and mottled. Watery eyes were bright blue behind thick glasses. He wore a stained and crumpled fedora. He was always playing the role of the cranky old-timer who was being put upon to examine corpses in situ, a role that he relished. Without a corpse to examine, he'd probably die of boredom.

Denny said, "Dad seems to be holding his own, Otis. He's tough, and the cancer seems to be in remission. Yup, he's still in Fort Lauderdale. How you been?"

"Great, Dennis. Can't complain. Tell your Dad I miss him. Whatta we got here? Another body. Jeez, I'm in a real recession-proof racket. Always stiffs to examine."

He turned to Rich. "You, yes, you. Plainclothes guy, shine your light right over the corpse and keep it steady, or you'll end up in the river. Denny, where do you get these punks?"

Rich, none too willingly, shone his large flashlight on the boy's body. Lanning donned latex gloves and slowly knelt down, bones creaking as he stooped. As he bent over, a fart escaped, a senior moment he might have been unaware of. If he was aware of it, he couldn't care less, because he used his age as an excuse for his crude behavior.

Par for the course, Denny thought.

Otis examined the head area and spent considerable time looking at the neck.

"You, light guy, bring your beam in closer here. Keep it steady. God, where do you get 'em, Denny? Losers all."

He lifted the boy's head and turned it so he could look at the back of the neck. He undid the buttons of the boy's fly, and pulled the pants down. The boy was beltless.

"Den, and you, light guy, help me turn him over. Hey, I didn't notice the good-looking gal back there. What's your name, honey?"

"Terry Kerrigan."

"Great. Watch out for these young guys. They get horny and start looking for you-know-what. Here, you guys, over now, easy."

After the body had been rolled over, the doctor slipped the boy's briefs down and inserted a thermometer in his anus.

"You, more light here. The neck! The neck! Not the ass. Jeez, Denny, where do you get these clowns anyway? Is there anybody left in the circus these days?"

Otis studied the back of the neck for several minutes. Then he ordered the body to be rolled over again to its original position. The examination took more than fifteen minutes.

He stood with the help of Denny and Rich. This time with Terry holding her flashlight, he wrote in his black notebook. He turned to her.

"Hon, you have nice hands. Use plenty of lotion in this kind of weather. Denny, when we get him on the table, we'll know more, but don't start asking time of death and the rest of the bullshit you dicks usually want to know. Preliminary—don't you dare quote me, or I'll kill you—I'd say strangulation. I think it was from behind. Nothing definite yet. Time of death, about eight to ten hours ago. I think, with the emphasis heavy on *think*, I think the homicide was committed somewhere else, and the body was dumped here."

As he got ready to leave he said, "Now, Den, take care of yourself. And you tell your dad that Otis is pulling for him and always will. He's a great guy. And light guy, you done good. You're going to go far with the cops. And little lady, if you ever want to have lunch and talk about skin-moisture remedies, Den has my number."

He turned and, with the help of his uniformed guide, picked his way back along the pier.

Rich said, "What a pain in the ass."

Denny replied, "Yeah, but one of the best when it comes to forensics."

Rich said, "He sure farts a lot."

Denny said to the others, "The body, rather than dumped, looks to me more like it was arranged, laid out like in a coffin. Almost a touch of reverence. Who found him?"

Rich said, "The big city car pound is next door. A worker from there wandered over to smoke a joint. He walked out on the pier, saw the body. Called it in from his cell. Then he heaved. His vomit is what you smell over there."

Denny said, "Should we call it a contaminated crime scene or just one that's all fucked up? C'mon, guys, let's go back to the car. It's getting cold out here."

Later, amid the squadron of police vehicles with their flashing lights, the three stood out on the street some people called Twelfth Avenue and others called West Street. They watched as the attendants loaded the body bag into the medical examiner's van.

Denny said, "Our first job is to see whether we can tie these three cases together. See if there are some common threads, correlations. No talking to the media, no mention of serial killers. We know nothing as yet. Rich, you haunt the lab people and crime techs for anything and everything. We coordinate with Central Homicide. I'm beginning to wonder if the murders of these three young guys will be of interest to the Sex Crimes Unit. Terry, please, get on the phone to them. These victims could be hustlers. Let's check drug use. Commonalities."

While Denny was midway through his instructions, Hal Madden, the veteran homicide detective, walked up. He greeted Denny. The jowly sergeant had worked with Denny on the murder case of Len Harrington, Denny's friend, the journalist who had written a book about Denny's involvement in the pursuit of the archterrorist, Felix the Cat. Madden was a sharp detective who had good instincts. He had stayed on beyond his retirement eligibility because of his widower status, his desire to remain busy and involved in life.

Madden said, "I have a gut feeling we're dealing with a serial killer. This looks like number three to me."

Denny replied, "Wait until the media gets a whiff of the words *serial killer*. Then we'll be working long days and nights on this."

Madden said, "Den, they may pitch this to your team. If I can be any help, let me know. You and your dad and me go back a long way, you know."

"I'll be sure to call on you, Hal."

Madden wandered off to talk to a uniformed captain who had shown up. When the uniformed brass smelled media attention, their antennae quivered.

Terry was driving north on the West Side Highway, Rich was sitting in the passenger seat talking quietly into his cell while Denny sat in the back looking out at the dark river beyond the highway. He was thinking back to the kid lying there, helpless, abandoned, lost forever to his world. Denny had seen many dead bodies before, even the shattered remains of people killed in terrorist bomb attacks, but this one seemed to hit him personally, get under his skin, into his gut.

He felt as if he were actually grieving for the boy, and yet he couldn't figure out why this particular victim had this dispiriting effect on him. He was close to tears, but why? Why this one? Why not one of the others? Perhaps he had seen him somewhere in life and didn't remember. Maybe he reminded him of someone. Maybe he reminded him of himself at that age. It was a strange nagging sadness, a kind of grief that enveloped him. He was snapped out of it by Terry's voice.

"Denny, Fazio is on the line and wants to talk to you. Lucky you."

"All I need now is some Pigmy shit."

2

The next morning Denny's team sat in their tiny office on the sixth floor of police headquarters at One Police Plaza, on Park Row across from City Hall in downtown Manhattan. They had two desks for the three of them, two filing cabinets, and five chairs—some wooden, some metal, no chair the same, all uncomfortable.

The nominal boss of the newly formed unit was Captain Alonzo Fazio, who was probably the shortest guy on the NYPD payroll. Behind his back people called him The Pigmy. People claimed he had worn elevator shoes in order to qualify for the police academy—if he had ever attended. He was a publicity-savvy cop who had had a rapid rise through the force. It looked like he was on the fast track for the police promotion ladder.

Fazio had sold the upper echelons on a special ops section that would investigate high-profile cases: art thefts, celebrities involved in crimes, cold cases that could benefit from twenty-first-century technological advances such as DNA, and pattern homicides. He had come up with the phrase *pattern homicides* to designate several killings that seemed to fit a pattern or a motif. Pattern homicides might be the beginning of something bigger, hopefully explained Fazio, not dreaded serial killings which were radioactive when picked up by the media, although he never fretted about too much media attention.

Fazio knew about Denny's close contacts with the media and his celebrity cop status, so he had talked his sponsors into tabbing Denny as the head of his special ops group. He asked Denny to choose a few compatible officers to form a squad.

The night of the most recent homicide discovery, Fazio had been notified by Central Homicide that a third body drop had shown up along the waterfront. He classified this as a pattern killing, and he had sent out Denny and his team to do a preliminary investigation.

In the tight office quarters, Denny was talking to Terry and Rich. Denny had his paper cup from Dunkin' Donuts, Terry had her Starbucks cup, and Rich had one from Seattle's Finest. They deliberately tried to bug each other with their different coffee choices.

Denny said, "Okay, let's see what we've got here. Okay, Terry, Number One. Name, age, pertinent details."

Terry replied, "I've been busy on the computer this morning. The autopsy on Number One wasn't very thorough because at first he was listed as a river floater so the case was given short shrift. He was buried in a potter's field grave because no one showed up to claim the body."

Denny said, "We should seek an exhumation. Gotta get Fazio to sign off on it. What was the guy's name?"

Terry said, "No ID so far. He was in his early twenties. Cause of death appeared to be strangulation but not a definite conclusion."

Denny asked, "Was Sex Crimes called out for an ID of this one?"

Terry said, "Don't know. I'll follow up on it."

"Have we got the in situ photos available?"

"Yes," she answered, "and I printed these out from the computer files."

Rich and Denny looked over her shoulder at the photos. The body had been laid out in a posed fashion just like the body they had seen on the pier. Flipping through the other photos, Denny could see it was a waterfront location, but other than that, there wasn't a great deal that the photos revealed. His youth was apparent.

Terry continued, "Victim Number Two, bingo on this one. In the autopsy records it turns out he had a condom stuffed in his mouth. Cause of death definite—strangulation. Death photos showed he was laid out like the latest one. His name was Collie Shreves."

Denny asked, "How do we know his name?"

She answered, "The family turned up to identify the body. They got a tip from someone on the phone. Didn't identify himself, just hung up. They went to the morgue and IDed the body."

Denny said, "Sounds kind of suspicious to me. It might have been the perp making sure he was getting his message across."

Terry said, "There's a lot more info on this one because Homicide was aware of the first body drop. Sex Crimes is checking on Number Two to see if he was known as a hustler."

Later the phone rang. Terry listened and took some notes.

After she hung up, she said, "Sex Crimes has identified Number Three, the latest one, our guy, from the death photos. They have him listed as a possible hustler. Name of Sean Walford. Had a couple of misdemeanors for loitering, had a drug problem.

"They have also confirmed that Number Two, Shreves, was working the streets, hustling to the best of their knowledge."

The door opened and Fazio came in, and said, "How's it going, guys? Tell me about last night."

He had a tic: pulling on the shoulder of his shirt as if the shirt were somehow too tight around the collar.

Denny summed up the details of what they had seen and all the pertinent information. Then Terry gave Fazio a rundown on the previous two body drops.

When he was told about the need for an autopsy on Number One, Fazio said, "I'm going to seek a court order for exhumation. Keep working on this, but for now, keep a low profile. We classify this as a *pattern homicide* until we get a complete autopsy on the first victim."

Denny said, "We're going to look at all these homicides and see if we can find correlations, relationships, commonalities among the cases."

"Coordinate with Sex Crimes," Pigmy said. "I know the boss over there, Lieutenant Marco, from way back, and I know he'll be very cooperative."

Inwardly Denny flinched at the idea of departmental cronyism—usually two wannabes pushing each other along up the ladder.

When Fazio left, Denny said, "So far The Pigmy seems ignited. Later he may even want to blow up all this into a serial-killer scenario. Then he can be seen on TV twenty-four/seven."

Terry said, "Yeah, but with all the Department's emphasis on counterterrorism, are the bigwigs gonna want a serial-killer mess dropped in their laps?"

Denny said, "No way. They hate serial killing. They're a cop's worst nightmare. Right now, guys, e-mail Sex Crimes the photos of Number One and see if they can match a name to the deceased."

Terry said, "One other thing, you probably already know. A few years ago Sex Crimes was split up. A separate larger unit deals with female abuse cases. That became a catchall section that incorporated all kinds of female abuse, rape cases, and later they more or less handled female prostitution cases, any other women's cases that years ago would be under the rubric of the Vice Squad.

"So today the Sex Crimes unit deals almost exclusively with stuff related to males. It was one of those restructuring deals that went through because of the Department's mishandling and lack of sensitivity on rape and family abuse cases. How female prostitution got lumped in is still a mystery. So, you figure."

Denny said, "Okay, then the experts on males should be in Sex Crimes. Those are the people we gotta see. In a way it's better to deal with specialists."

3

Denny and Monny were always happy to be living in Manhattan. Except for occasional visits to Fort Lauderdale to see his folks, they were satisfied roaming around the city. When they tired of the city, they'd rent a car and drive upstate, out to Long Island, to Jersey, even down to New Hope, Pennsylvania. Basically they were city creatures who could visit museums, wander around Central Park, take the subway to favorite spots like down to South Ferry where they'd board the Staten Island ferry for a harbor ride.

Often they'd trek to South Street Seaport, the West Village, Soho—wherever. They had just discovered the High Line, running between Tenth and Eleventh Avenue, the park-garden built on abandoned elevated railroad tracks from Gansevoort Street to West Twentieth Street.

The city in its infinite variety was a challenge to them. They were always discovering new areas, new neighborhoods, new restaurants, bars, art galleries, stores, bakeries, delis, libraries—anything urban that struck their fancy.

They'd grab a subway or a bus to God knows where—to Fort Tryon Park, the Bronx Zoo, the Brooklyn Botanical Gardens.

The city was their oyster, their playground, their Northwest Passage, their Open Sesame. It always had been and would be their infinite and endless kingdom for discovery, serendipity, and wonderment.

On a dreary October Sunday, Denny and his wife were having brunch in the Thalia on Eighth Avenue at West Fiftieth Street. Denny and his team had been cut loose temporarily from the case of the kid found on the Hudson River pier. Before they could get involved, Central Homicide had to decide if there was a link among the various homicides. The

Department had an aversion to serial-killer cases. These spooked the public, provoked a media frenzy, and most of all were a bitch to solve.

One reason serial-killer crimes were difficult to solve, Denny knew, was that murderer and victims were often unknown to each other. Murders of strangers by strangers. The victim might be part of a category rather than someone the perp knew. The victim perhaps filled the killer's profile target rather than being a family member, friend or neighbor. Anonymity between killer and prey meant an essential element would be missing in the investigation. The investigators couldn't look among the relatives and circle of people known to the victim, but had to look among the public at large. The victim was prey rather than someone familiar to the killer.

For that day's matinee Denny had been given house seats to the straight play *August: Osage County*. He and Monica were Broadway theater junkies, and there was little they didn't know about the Great White Way. Usually they saw almost every new show within weeks of its opening, but somehow they had not yet seen the Tracy Letts play.

Monica had read the text and had reviewed it for Amazon, giving it five stars. She said it took her a second reading to really appreciate the play. Both of them were looking forward to seeing it. Dysfunctional families were so much fun to watch from the outside, so rotten to experience from within.

They were also looking forward to seeing *Equus* as well as *Billy Elliot*, both London hits, in a few weeks. Monny said she couldn't wait to see Daniel Radcliffe, aka Harry Potter, in the altogether in *Equus*. Denny's reply had been the typical, usually female, response, "If you've seen one, you've seen 'em all."

Monica was spreading the pieces of her eggs Benedict around on the plate to take advantage of the hollandaise sauce. She tried to spear egg white, a piece of Canadian bacon, a hunk of English muffin and a smear of egg yolk and rich sauce onto her fork.

She said, "Did you hear about *Hairspray*?"

"No, uh-uh."

"They announced it's closing in January. Harvey Fierstein is coming back in November to reprise his Edna role before it closes."

"How long has it been open?"

"Your mother says six years."

Denny's mother was a longtime theater maven since the time she'd worked for the Shuberts. Monny and her mother-in-law, Carole Delaney in Fort Lauderdale, swapped e-mails every day, and the two of them gave each other all the inside theater dope.

Monny had a good job at Smith Barney, but with the financial upheaval going on, no one knew what was going to happen from day to day. For the past few years she had been running a very popular blog which generated a lot of buzz and controversy. Monica didn't mince words, said it like it was and damn the consequences. Denny was proud of her and got a kick out of the fuss she stirred up. She was adept at ruffling feathers, blog-style.

Denny asked, "Hon, I didn't get a chance to look at your blog today. What's cooking?"

"Den, today on the blog it's the runaway poppy trade in Afghanistan, the pros and cons of the Wall Street bailout plan that Congress passed, Bloomberg's end run around term limits to get a third term as mayor, the bad unemployment numbers, the way Paulson screwed up by not bailing out Lehmann Brothers early on, and the crisis in Pakistan. Want to hear more?"

"No, Monny, I think that's more than my brain can handle right now."

"There's a lot more stuff."

Denny's cell vibrated in his pocket.

"Excuse me, hon."

It was Terry Kerrigan. Denny knew that she was not one of Monica's favorite people because Terry's good looks and availability had caused a bit of marital slippage in the past.

Terry and Denny had had a one-night stand that could have led to disaster. Monny might have suspected, but Denny never knew for sure.

Terry said, "Denny, Captain Fazio got the court exhumation order for Number One."

"What's our status?"

"Pigmy wants us to stand down until they can tie all three cases together. We can't do anything until after the exhumation. He said to keep working the cases as if we're assigned, but to keep as low a profile as we can manage. As soon as we get the go-ahead, he wants us to meet with Sex Crimes."

"Okay, thanks, keep me up to date."

"Will do."

He flipped off his cell and pocketed it.

Terry had noticed he didn't use her name, and she guessed he was with Monica.

Monica said, "Is the theater still on, or have you been called in?"

"No, no problems. It's a go."

When they walked into the theater and saw the curtainless stage, they had time to study the details of the three-story house set. Elaborate stuff cluttered the first-floor rooms.

Monny commented, "A great set. I love it."

After seeing the three acts of *August, Osage County*, they both felt wrung out. The play was well written and well acted with a lot of humor, zingers that kept the audience roaring, but the family battles were intense.

Monny said, "This play just proves how much acting talent is on view in New York."

4

Denny's squad had been made operational and placed in charge of the river homicides because the powers that be had deemed the case the work of a serial killer. As the media started circling the departmental wagons, some of the brass began to panic. A nut was on the loose, a killer with a cause and a brain, the worst kind, someone who might fold his tent and wait for a decade or longer to strike again or even move to California and begin again with another MO. It was like a bad dream, the worst case scenario.

When the media got out the word that a serial killer was on the loose, all hell broke out. The uniformed brass in the Department went to the mattresses and laid low. They weren't about to take the heat. That's what underlings, the guys they referred to as the field hands, were for.

Denny, Rich, and Terry had gathered in a back office at Central Homicide after the exhumation. Though Denny's special squad had been set up to investigate unique homicide cases, he had hoped it wouldn't be a serial-killer case. His team hadn't been given any yet, but they were the toughest to crack.

This one would fit their mandate if it turned out to be a serial killer. At its inception Denny had been asked whom he wanted on his team, and he immediately chose Rich and Terry. It was best to work with people you knew well, partners who would watch your back. They were both bright and well trained with good cop instincts.

Terry said, "Number One had a condom in his mouth just like the others. The original autopsy never found it, so now we know all three are part of a pattern. The medical examiner is not going to rebury Number One at present. Also they said strangulation is a more-definite possibility. They're putting him in a locker and keeping him in storage in case something else comes to light.

"We checked. The condoms were manufactured in Malaysia. They make hundreds of millions of them, and they're shipped everywhere. Our perp could have picked up a handful in any number of spots. They're giveaways—in gay and lesbian centers, health clinics, parenthood places, singles clubs, swinger places, and gay places like guest houses, baths, bookstores, bars, you name it. Everywhere but at baby showers and bar and bat mitzvahs."

"Could a list of outlets be of any use to us?"

"Nada. It would be such a long list it'd be useless."

"What about batch numbers, codes, manufacturing dates?" Denny asked.

"We can try, but the major distributor said it would be impossible. The three we recovered from the bodies have no identifying dates, codes or anything. The distributor said that usually the big bags they come in are marked, coded, and dated, but the individual condoms aren't. It's an enormous market. This type costs practically nothing to make, and they're not sold. They're freebies."

Rich asked, "What does a condom in the victim's mouth mean? Are we looking for a guy or woman who caught HIV/AIDS from a hustler, and now it's payback time?"

Denny said, "Possible. It could be a signature."

"But why a condom?" asked Rich.

"Because it connotes sex, intercourse. It's a talisman. It could mean unprotected sex is a no-no."

Terry said, "Den, we've got an ID on Number One. His name is Benjamin Moore."

"Are you shitting me? That's the name of a paint company, for Christ sake. It's a brand name. Next one will be Sherwin Williams."

"No, I'm not kidding you. That's the guy's name."

"Have you run the name through our computers."

"Yup. Nothing of a criminal nature showed up."

"Then how did you get a make on this victim?"

"He'd been fingerprinted before serving a brief stint in the navy. The Department of Defense came up with a match. He was honorably discharged under the 'don't ask, don't tell policy.' After he was in the service for a while, he told them he was gay and got thrown out. Probably got sick of the service and knew what to say to get out."

Denny said, "Okay, guys, we've got to make a chart with these three victims, all the information we've gathered, as much data as possible. Again, we've got to look for connections, commonalities."

Terry said, "I'm wondering if these three victims were pre-selected or picked out randomly. What if this guy has a list he's working off of?"

At that moment The Pigmy came into the office.

He said, "Shit. I just came from media relations. They're worried that this thing is going to blow up into something too big. We may have opened up the genie's bottle here, and we won't be able to get the cap back on again. Denny, I'm going to need you to keep your ears open to your media sources. See what they know."

Fazio paced around the room for a few minutes and then stared at the three team members.

"Damn. I may have to call in the cavalry for this. Get ready for the perfect storm on this one. Denny and guys, give this a full-court press. Use every resource. Beat the bushes. Put this on the front burner. Let me know if you need any court orders, and I'll expedite them for you. Burn rubber. Den, you're the best. Give it your all, your best shot. Terry and Rich, you've got my full support."

After he had exhausted all of his formulaic exhortations, he turned abruptly and went out of the office slamming the door. The little general had spoken and was now going back to hunker in his bunker, thought Denny.

Denny said, "Why do I feel like it's a locker room at half-time? There's a guy who loves publicity, but can't stand the heat. Publicity hounds are all the same. Praising a fallen hero is easy for them, but they know getting caught up in a serial-killing swamp can be frightening because no one knows where it can lead, how long the case will last, and how to extricate themselves if they get dragged down by media criticism.

"We've got to lay out a game plan on this, and we have to expect more homicides unless this guy has finished his job."

Terry said, "Do you think there's a possibility he killed two of them to cover up the one he was really after?"

"Don't know. A possibility, but I doubt it. And was he pissed off because his condom signature went unnoticed on Victim Number One? The only reason for the condoms would be to call attention to the fact the murders are related, part of a pattern. Some kind of a crusade."

Rich said, "Does he go after hustlers because he's a serial killer, or is he after them in particular for some deep-seated psychological reason?"

Denny answered, "I don't think anybody but an absolute nutcase sets out to be a serial killer. I see this as an obsession to wipe out some hustlers because he hates them as a group, but he may even have a list of those he's going to eliminate. He's got this fixation right now to act against them. It's going to keep him going until the need to kill abates."

5

Denny, Rich, Hal Madden and Terry were sitting in Lieutenant Marco's Sex Crimes conference room. Denny had brought along Hal Madden of Central Homicide to sit in on the meeting so he'd be up to speed on the investigation. To Denny the space smelled like a ripe locker room, and he thought he caught the whiff of poppers, or was it essence of dirty gym socks or sweaty jockstraps that he caught? Some pervasive smell, maybe the sour smell of sex gone bad. Appropriate for a sex crimes office, Denny supposed.

In the cramped office space were Lieutenant Marco, head of the Central Manhattan Sex Crimes unit, his face flushed, his neck bursting out of his tight collar. With him sat two of his men, Sergeants Harley Stennis and Jerry Slattery, detectives who focused on the gay scene. Denny knew both were sharp street cops, not desk jockeys. They had good reputations.

Stennis was outgoing. Slattery was reticent, quieter. About Slattery, Terry had said before the meeting, "He's a stunner. Incredibly good-looking, movie star looks. Like Paul Newman in his prime with those piercing blue eyes."

Stennis was in his sixties. He'd stayed on long after his retirement eligibility. Denny wondered why. *Other guys would have been burned out by this time.* Slattery appeared to be in his forties. Both men looked like they worked out, kept in shape. Glancing at Slattery's blue eyes, Denny was reminded of what Terry had said: they were a mesmerizing blue.

Denny said, "I'd appreciate it if you guys could just give us a background on hustlers and johns so that we have a general idea of what we're looking for."

Stennis began, "One thing I think you guys should know

right off the bat—most johns prefer straight guys, or ones they think are straight, or guys that act straight. Most of them want one-way sex, lay-backs. They want to be in charge and usually give oral sex. If you're paying a guy, you don't have to have him back unless you want to pay him the next time. It's easy to write tricks off that way.

"Many johns are turned off by gay guys. It's part of their fantasy that they are having it off with a young straight guy. They are conquerors and know or think they're getting heterosexual guys. Most of the time, gays scare them off, because in their own minds, johns don't consider themselves gay.

"I think a lot of cops make a mistake of equating johns and hustlers with johns and female prostitutes. I think they're two entirely different worlds. A certain percentage of hustlers are gay or bisexual. And I believe being bisexual is a reality, not a myth.

"Johns can pretend that a certain hustler is straight if it looks like it will benefit them. I think a lot of johns are like adolescent boys. They've never grown up emotionally or sexually. Because they may be straight guys in their own minds, they are just fooling around, touching another kid's genitalia with nothing gay involved.

"Maybe they have low self-worth, low self-esteem. Hey, I'm not a psychologist, but we've interviewed hundreds of these johns."

Denny thought to himself how many johns being interviewed by cops give away too much of the inner workings of their minds. And how much would they know about their inner workings anyway? He'd be willing to bet that Stennis had done a lot of reading on the subject, probably spoken to psychologists, attended workshops, and been given insights that he had internalized.

Stennis went on, "It's a fantasy, a dream world. They're playing games to get their rocks off. They're producing a play in their own minds, directing it, telling the actors what to do, how to do it, setting the stage, sometimes doing the costuming. They make up the plots in their heads.

"Delaney, I think your guy is pissed off. He's carrying it a step further. He's gone beyond the games stage into other territory. Maybe it's retribution, or maybe even salvation he's seeking.

"Back to johns in general: they don't mind if the trick has a girlfriend. That proves that the trick is straight. They got their straight ticket stamped and validated. The tricks can even be married and have kids. Hey, that just shows they're real men.

"Being or acting butch is prized. They don't want feminine guys. Johns usually don't want the tricks to make any sexual moves or overtures. They usually don't want, perhaps even fear two-way reciprocation. They don't want feminine types, sure, but usually they don't want gays in general.

"In their own minds many feel they're not gay. That's a dirty word. Usually they don't want to be seen with a gay guy who is obviously gay."

Denny wondered if it was always the way Stennis said it was. Stennis did all the talking while Slattery and Marco sat silently. Dennis was listening carefully, and Rich and Terry were taking notes. Stennis was a gold mine of information.

Stennis was on a roll: "Johns don't want a relationship. That scares them. The hustler might be gay. Conquest is when you can get a straight guy. It's no real challenge to get a gay hustler. The worst crime a hustler can commit, no matter how buffed he is, is to act *queeny*.

"From the get-go, let me fill you in on what I believe. You could be looking for an executioner on a mission, but why does he only pick on hustlers?

"I think since all of the victims we believe were hustlers, then I think you're looking for a john. I'll tell you why."

I bet you will, thought Denny.

Stennis went on and on, "If the perp was just picking off young guys, if he was just trolling the streets, looking for young male hustlers, he'd find more young guys hanging around pushing drugs. There are way more young pushers than hustlers today on the streets. Probably a hell of a lot more money in it and a hell of a lot less risk. None of these victims were serious drug pushers or users. Maybe a little recreational stuff, but that wasn't their bag, okay? So let's say our guy was selecting, choosing hustlers, deliberately and solely.

"Only a john would know who was who, who to look for, where to look for them, and what to say to them to get them into a vehicle. A drug-pushing kid ain't going to get in a car. Why should he? He's making a sale of a substance, not himself. He'd be an idiot to get in some stranger's car. The pusher might have a lot of money on him and some dope besides. The guy in the car could be trying to rip him off. A pusher would do all of his business from outside the car, not inside."

Denny offered, "Unless the meeting takes place on the Internet or over the phone, and the kid goes to the killer's place. The kid might have answered a come-on invitation on the Web."

"Yeah, that's a possibility, but again it leads you to a john, not a random killer—at least that's what I think."

"Okay, agreed. But what's in it for the john, to be killing these kids?"

Stennis said, "Hey, Lieutenant, that's your job to figure out all this shit, not ours. That's way above our pay grade—right Slattery?"

Slattery merely nodded.

Denny said, "This has been an eye-opener for me. The more background you can give us on the hustler-john scene, the better we'll be equipped to handle this case. With you guys as part of the team, of course."

Stennis began his narrative again. "Okay, Lieutenant, let me clue you in on some other stuff. Some johns are ugly or think they are. Some of them came out late in life. Some are anxious about the way their bodies look, or their penis size, too small or too ugly. Many are self-conscious, don't believe in themselves sexually although they may have been very successful in life doing things, making money. Some are fatties. Some are incredibly cheap. That seems to go with the territory. Others, though, are very generous. They'll pay hundreds for a session.

"Some have very strange lives. Some like to live frugally, living on a can of Campbell's soup or going to McDonald's all the time. They come in all types and sizes.

"Some are real loners, have no friends other than other johns. They're a strange breed. In a sense your guy may have gone from being a sexual predator to being a killer-predator, not such a stretch for some of these freaks."

Denny wished he could get Slattery into the conversation, but he was afraid to break into Stennis's flow of information.

Stennis took a break and said, "I was on the force when the old hustler bars were still going strong. There was the Haymarket on Eighth Avenue between West Forty-seventh and Forty-eighth. Cowboys was one of the busiest hustler bars on the East side, on East Fifty-third between First and Second Avenues.

"Truman Capote and Tennessee Williams were in Cowboys holding court all the time. And after that closed, came Rounds on the same street about a half block away and on the opposite side and east of Cowboys. Across from the shuttered Cowboys was a little hole in the wall with bleachers called Le Bar, another hustler joint.

"In the nineteen eighties there used to be a joint on Fourteenth Street called Ritzie's. For a time the kids would take the E train. It was called the Hustler Local. The toy boys would hit the bars on East Fifty-third, buzz into the Haymarket in the West Forties on Eighth Avenue, and then touch base with the one on Fourteenth and Eighth, in the Village—all of the bars on the E line. You'd see the same johns and the same tricks in all three places within a couple of hours. It was like the old Silk Route in the Orient. Only this one was the Jockey shorts route with skid marks."

Denny thought, *This guy is too full of old information that has nothing to do with nineteen-year-olds or kids or in their early twenties working the streets today.*

But Stennis kept going, and Denny didn't try to interrupt him because there might be some nuggets in amongst the dross.

"In the old days there was Dirty Edna's in Times Square, the Loading Zone on the East Side. Oh, so many. In the West Village there was the basement of the Ninth Circle on West Tenth with Uncle Paul's at the corner of Greenwich Avenue. Even Julius's had its hustler regulars. Lots of street action in the East Fifties."

Oh, my God, this guy is going to start reaching into the Great Depression and gay speakeasies pretty soon.

Marco spoke up for the first time and said, "Stennis is a goddamn encyclopedia or Wickipedia of hustler life."

Denny said to Stennis, "Look, Harley, what I need is a rundown on contemporary hustler activity. No offense, but we have to realize that the kids playing the streets today don't know about hustling in the seventies, eighties, and nineties. They were in elementary school in the nineties. I need help on the kids and johns that are around now. What we're looking for are correlations, connections, commonalities among these three homicides."

Stennis laughed. "I was just trying to give you a little history."

Slattery spoke for the first time, "Since HIV/AIDS the number of hustlers has gone way down. Too risky. A scary lifestyle. Good economic times have a lot to do with the number of hustlers. When there are plenty of jobs, hustlers disappear. This present economic downturn may cause a big new influx. If it weren't for drug usage, the number of hustlers would be far less, but some of these guys have to get money from somewhere to support their expensive habits so they have to turn tricks. They'll do anything to make a buck."

Denny watched Terry scoping out Slattery, who did have piercing blue eyes. Denny thought Slattery looked depressed and withdrawn. Maybe this homicide case was dragging him down.

Rich said, "They're not all into drugs, are they?"

Stennis added, "No, and you got the occasional amateur out there looking for kicks. And a lot of the business guys are gays who enjoy it. And bisexual kids. Some kids would, pardon the expression, fuck a snake. Excuse me, Terry, but that's the way it is."

Terry said, "Hey, Stennis, you don't have to watch your language with me. I grew up in Hell's Kitchen, not in some little hick town."

Denny said to the group, "Now we have to formulate a plan of action. If you guys from Sex Crimes will give us a rundown on the current crop of johns and hustlers and keep your ears and eyes open for any signs of a predator, we would deeply appreciate it."

Denny noticed by his body language that Lieutenant Marco resented him, a fellow lieutenant taking over, giving orders to his crew. Marco, Denny sensed, could be an obstructionist protecting his sacred territory.

Stennis and Slattery agreed to make up lists of the hustlers and johns they knew were active.

Slattery said, "My theory, for what it's worth, is that we may be looking for a perp who isn't a regular. Someone who just happens to stumble on these kids, maybe because they're on the streets looking to be picked up."

Denny added, "You guys could also help us by clueing us in on which of the victims were known to you, and what you knew about them. What were their habits, their hangouts?"

Marco said, "And everybody, let's keep the channels of communication open here. Make sure that I'm informed of everything, and I mean everything that affects my squad and my personnel. Let's stay aware of chain of command and areas of responsibility. No one should go off half-cocked, lone ranger-style, in this investigation. Are we agreed?"

Denny thought the expression "half-cocked" was ironic in the context of what they had been discussing.

At the end Denny regarded Marco as too conscious of his own turf. He could get in the way of a thorough investigation.

The Department was loaded with these feudal lords protecting their fiefdoms. And Denny remembered that the Pigmy knew Marco, and the two probably kept in touch.

On the way back to their base, Denny said, "It's a jungle out there, guys. And without Stennis to encapsulate the whole history of gay life for us, we might get trapped and set upon by pythons and alligators. But our main problem is going to be departmental brass swinging from tree to tree over our heads, and crony quicksand under our feet."

6

Denny was seated at his kitchen table reading a Maureen Dowd column in the *Times*. Sometimes she hit a homer out of the ballpark. This time she had struck out. She wasn't even funny. His landline phone rang.

"Denny, how've you been?"

That unmistakable nasal twang, his old nemesis, Bruce Wexler, head of the New York FBI field office since before Nine-Eleven. How had Wexler been able to keep his job so long despite scores of screwups? Probably because he so willingly fell on the sword and had become the fall guy for higher-ups. He had become a sieve from so many sword entries, mea culpas. Years ago Denny had dubbed him The Ferret, and the name had stuck with the media, much to Wexler's dismay.

"Senior Agent-in-Charge Wexler? Good to hear from you, bro. I've been okay. How 'bout you? What's up, buddy?"

"Denny, could we meet somewhere for lunch, for a talk?"

In itself that was unusual. In the past it had always been a summons to The Ferret's office. Maybe he wanted a job recommendation. Perhaps he wanted to be a night security guard at Macy's. Perhaps he'd ask for a theater freebie. A house seat for *Billy Elliot* or *Wicked*?

"Sure. We could meet. How about the Polish Tea Room in the Edison Hotel on West Forty-seventh? You know, the coffee shop off the lobby. A couple of blocks away from where Felix the Cat nailed you that time. You know, the time you almost bought the farm? You remember the occasion when he shot you on the street outside The Palm steak house?"

Denny loved to rub it in, get under The Ferret's skin. Make his balls itch. He noticed the brief moments of silence while Wexler tried to recover from what Denny had said. Theirs was a great working relationship built on a foundation of mutual distrust and dislike.

After a momentary lull in the conversation while The Ferret tried to recapture his aplomb, he said, "One thirty okay for you, Denny?"

"Sure. I'll be in the back. Past the counter, in the back on the left."

"See you."

Denny was puzzled. He wondered if Wexler had something to share about the river homicides. If it turned into a serial-killer case, the NYPD might want to use the FBI's Offender profiling capabilities, share use of the Quantico expertise.

Later Denny was waiting for Wexler in the Edison Café, located in the Edison Hotel which had been built in 1931 with many art deco touches. He looked around his favorite hangout known as the Polish Tea Room. It was spread out over a large space in the former pre–World War II ballroom of the hotel that still had some of its faded glory and touches of an ornate past, with high vaulted ceilings and decorative pillars and walls. Big tacky hand-lettered signs had been posted around the space, some addressed to customers and some to the help.

It had lots of Jewish deli fare including matzo ball soup, pastrami, corned beef sandwiches, chopped liver, lox, white-fish, blintzes and other standard fare, along with plenty of comfort food. It had a more-ornate seediness than its basic Polish-Jewish food or than a coffee shop had a right to possess. One alcove was always roped off for playwrights, producers, and actors. Denny called it the August Wilson annex because the playwright had often done some of his writing there.

The help was always standoffish and offhanded until they got to know you. Even then you had to walk on tiptoe. They were very efficient but cold to the touch. The same waiters and waitresses had been working there for years. Orders were shouted out through the open window space to the kitchen, and a waiter might be heard yelling to the bus boy, "Three waters for Number Sixteen."

On a wall near Denny was an unframed poster for Neil

Simon's *45 Seconds from Broadway* which featured the café as its setting. Denny and Monny had seen it during its brief Broadway run and had enjoyed the stand-up comedian in it who was like Jackie Mason.

At one twenty Wexler walked into the café and spotted Denny at a back table. The crowd was thin, so they would not have to worry about eavesdroppers. They shook hands and exchanged phony hearty greetings.

Denny ordered a swiss on pumpernickel to go with the iced tea he was nursing. Wexler ordered a chopped liver on a kaiser, a side of cole slaw, french fries, and a diet Coke.

After some fake chitchat, Wexler began, "Den, have you heard about the Felix graffiti that's been turning up around the city?"

"No, I haven't."

"Yeah, someone has been spraying 'Felix is Back' all over Manhattan. Mostly on street surfaces. At first we thought it was some kid, a prank, a joke, some black humor, but it was very persistent. Civilians were and are getting antsy about it. It could be harmless, but it's gotten to be more than an annoyance.

"A few nights ago witnesses saw an SUV pull up at a street corner in the East Sixties. A guy in his forties gets out and spray paints 'Felix is Back' using a big stencil. He hurries back to the SUV, gets in the passenger seat, and it takes off like a big-ass bird. The wits couldn't tell the make or model. They didn't catch the plate numbers, but now we know it's not the work of kids. We've done studies of all the graffiti, and they're all the work of one guy or one outfit."

"Okay, fine, but is this something I can do anything about? Are members of Felix's cell doing it?"

"Denny, I just want to keep you in the loop on this, keep you in the frame. We're doing everything we can to track down these graffiti guys. So far, we haven't tied it down to anything else, and the media hasn't picked up on it in any big way.

"But, Denny, there's something much more alarming than

the Felix graffiti. Now, let me tell you about something a hell of a lot more serious. A week ago authorities apprehended a suicide bomber wearing an explosive vest like the kind they use in Iraq."

"Oh, shit, a suicide bomber? Has this hit the media?"

"No, we're keeping this close to our vests for now. Uh-oh, wrong word. I don't have to tell you what a panic this could cause. Here's how it all went down. At the Forty-second Street entrance to Grand Central, the one by Vanderbilt Avenue, a cop sees this suspicious guy hanging around. The guy looks at the cop. Panic in his eyes. Fear. Something just wasn't right about him. He's wearing a long heavy overcoat on a warm day. He's sweating like a pig. Looks at the cop, is shaking. The cop nods at his partner. They move in on the guy and take him from both sides. They took a big chance, but the cop smelled something fishy. The guy freezes.

"He says, 'I didn't mean to do it.' 'Do what?' the cop says. 'Kill people,' says the guy in the overcoat. He falls on his knees. They search him. See the vest. Cuff him. All hell breaks loose. They call for help. Other cops clear the streets, the whole terminal. The bomb squad comes. They hustle the guy into a bomb truck, haul him away. The guy passes out. They get the vest off of him. Later that day they blow up the vest. It turns out it was a powerful bomb he could have set off inside the terminal, maybe even where Felix the Cat planted his first one. Full of shrapnel, nails, ball bearings, all that crap. Big explosive charge. Real heavy shit.

"It would have been devastating. The cops deserve medals. We've been interrogating the bomber ever since, but I don't want to get into that right now. I'm mainly trying to keep you abreast of developments just in case we call on you, okay?"

Denny said, "I appreciate that. Was this guy operating alone?"

"Probably a homegrown guy, but, Den, I can't get into that right now. But we may need you on this later as things develop. The bomb was a carbon copy of the kind used by suicide-vest bombers in Iraq. We checked it out with the CIA and DOD. One reason why I'm clueing you in on this: the guy has heard of you, admires you. We may need you later. He may be willing to talk to you. In fact, you may be the only one he'll talk to. He's specifically asked for you."

"I've got an awful lot on my plate right now, but I'll be glad to help if you think I can do any good."

After Wexler told Denny more about the apprehended terrorist, he switched to another topic so Denny wouldn't probe too much. "I hear you have a serial killer on your case load. We'll be glad to help you with our profiling unit."

"Yeah, we'll be calling on the Bureau if it goes in that direction, but you know how the NYPD brass hates you guys."

"Probably with good reason. Everybody's always watching his own rice bowl."

Denny thought this was a different Wexler than he had known in the past.

Wexler smiled and said, "I love Monny's blog."

"Are you a regular reader?"

"Oh, yeah, for sure. She can really stir the pot, get people hepped up. I love to read the stuff she digs up. Do you get any static from the Department about her blog?"

"No, why should I?"

"She cuts awfully close to the bone in her comments at times. You know how bureaucracies are. Sensitive, gun-shy, overly concerned about public reaction, repercussions."

"Jeez, that almost describes you, doesn't it?"

Wexler had learned to ignore some of Denny's digs.

Denny continued, "But I guess that's why she does it. If she didn't bust balls now and then, why do it? What fun would there be in blandness? It's her outlet."

"Do you contribute?"

"Uh-uh. It's all hers. I have my own anti-FBI blog that keeps me busy."

"Are you kidding me?"

"Why should I kid you? It's called www dot fbiscrewup dot org."

"You wish."

"No, blogging doesn't interest me. To me, it's boring, too time-consuming, but Monny likes it, so fine. I want her to be her own person, do her own thing. Talking to a computer screen is dull. I'd rather do the Sunday *Times* crossword puzzles or knit doilies than run a blog."

They parted shortly after. Denny thought, *Cripes, a Felix connection. Felix always returns smelling like a bad turd. Felix graffiti! And a suicide-vest bomber no less. Does Wexler ever have any good news to spread?*

Denny noticed that Wexler didn't have anything to contribute on the riverside killings. He probably didn't see it as an FBI priority as yet since they hadn't been called in.

Denny walked back home along Forty-sixth thinking about the vest bomber and the Felix graffiti people. Hell, life was a bitch, and added to all this was his serial-killer case, the river homicides. He'd have no time for Wexler's stuff. He wondered why Wexler had bothered to fill him in on things beyond Denny's control, but the vest bomber's interest in him caused him concern. Why should a terrorist be interested in him?

7

The news that Denny would be leading a team to investigate the murders of some hustlers didn't take long to leak out, and, of course, Denny once again came under a great deal of media attention and scrutiny, some of it negative. Several newspapers, TV outlets and Web sites had dug out profiles of him.

One of Denny's unfavorite media people, Packy Pucker, wrote a column on him for the *Post*.

DENNY DELANEY IS AT IT AGAIN!

One of the media's darlings, Denny Delaney, intrepid investigator for the NYPD and FBI, Dick Tracy reincarnated, will be getting a lot of attention from his press buddies again. He'll be basking in the limelight once more. He has always liked hobnobbing in the watering holes of Broadway with the rich and famous and the media elite, with anyone who might further his career in the NYPD.

He became famous in his pursuit of that infamous terrorist scum, Felix the Cat. Denny had the good fortune of killing Felix not once, but twice. The first time in the dank, dismal, dark tunnels below Grand Central Station and the second time in a Forty-second Street movie house. I'm not going into all that right now, but if you're that interested, Google it and find out the intriguing details of how super–sleuth Delaney tracked down a nutcase terrorist—not once but twice. How lucky can you get?

One of Delaney's fearless feckless feats was riding at breakneck speed on the back of a commandeered police motorcycle down Broadway and through Bryant Park chasing Felix. I kid you not. Of course he didn't catch the furtive felonious feline that time, but the unlucky motorcycle cop ended up with serious back injuries and a disability pension.

In the Felix case Denny was battling incipient alcoholism that almost cost him his career, a career incidentally which benefited from his father's years on the force. His dad was an outstanding officer, as he was gladly willing to impart in the same Great White Way pit stops frequented by his son. When celebrities came to town, it was the elder Delaney's task to squire them around town while supposedly supplying VIP security, and that included visiting heads of state and even popes.

I know Denny has gone through some tough periods. One was the time when his buddy and my friend, the real pro newsman, Len Harrington, was murdered by Felix II. Len and Denny had collaborated on a book entitled Nine Lives, Two Men. It was about Denny's relentless hunt for Felix I which ended up with Felix I's alleged death in Grand Central on a subway track, when Denny, in order to protect himself, was forced to thrust Felix into a death by electrocution on the third rail. Of course, there were no immediate witnesses to this deserved death.

Then Felix II killed Harrington in retaliation for the book and a movie being filmed in Manhattan. It was Felix II's way of getting back at Denny. Harrington was a great guy and a fantastic investigative reporter.

Now here is Denny back again to Gotham's rescue, in the public spotlight, this time in pursuit of a serial killer who is eliminating male hustlers and depositing their bodies along the waterfront. We wish Denny well. (Uh, kinda, except when he's being a publicity hound.)

What's this we hear about another attempted bombing in Grand Central? Don't tell me it's Felix Redux, perhaps Felix III. I thought we had DNA proof that he was gone forever. If you know anything about this new bombing attempt, give me a tweet. And don't forget all that "Felix is Back" stuff that's being painted all over our streets. What's with all that anyway? Will we ever get a full explanation of all this bullcrap? I doubt it.

Denny's long-suffering gorgeous spouse Monica runs that breathy, bratty, bristling blog that is daring and racy. She accompanies her fearless sleuthing hubby on his rounds of the Times Square public houses in his relentless pursuit of publicity.

When Felix I's first bomb went off in Grand Central that horrific day, Denny was almost blasted into oblivion. That's when the FBI called upon him as their savior. Remember Agent Bruce Wexler, dubbed The Ferret, how he chose Denny to join the investigation? Why choose Denny in the first place? How Denny managed his case-load while juggling his liquor intake was a miracle.

Let us also recall that at one time before the second death of Felix, the FBI minions led by The Ferret had Felix II in the hoosegow, and he was being interrogated by none other than Detective Delaney. Somehow, never made clear to the public or media, Felix escaped and was on the loose to do further damage.

One night in Sardi's Denny took a swing at me, but I was saved by some of his off-duty detective buddies. When he reads this column, he's going to really go after me. Hey, Dennis, I've got a sharp lawyer, so I'd love to sue you.

Dennis, a Fordham grad, is of the new school of cops, college–educated and savvy, not like the old rubber-hose-wielding Neanderthals of the past. He

and Monny are theater buffs and see all the latest shows, probably on freebies presented to him by his theater cronies.

A frequenter of the joints on Restaurant Row, Dennis can often be spotted in the street's food emporiums.

No, but truly, I wish Dennis good luck on this new case and hope for the best. Let's just hope that Felix III is not on the prowl.

Denny was at his desk in Central Homicide reading the column, growing more furious by the moment, when the landline telephone rang. He tore the page from the paper and pocketed it.

"Is this Lieutenant Dennis Delaney?"

"Yes."

"Hi, my name is Tim."

"May I ask your last name?"

"Not right now. Just Tim will have to do."

"Okay, what can I do for you, Tim?"

"I've read about you, seen you on TV. You're the head honcho investigating the murders, the bodies found along the riverfront, aren't you?"

"Yes, I am."

"I knew two of those guys who were found."

"Which two?"

"One you identified as Sean Walford. The latest one. I knew him, and I knew one of the other guys whose body was found. His name was Collie."

"Did you know his last name?"

"I only knew him as Collie. Are you tracing this call?"

"No, we're not."

"Yeah, I bet. Anyway it's a throwaway cell I found, so it won't do you any good."

"Where did you know these two guys from?"

"We used to hang out together. Nothing really close. We'd meet, have coffee, gab a little, compare notes."

"Notes about what?"

"Mainly about johns. Which ones were okay, which ones were scumbags, bad apples, cheapskates, crooks who wouldn't pay what they'd promised, ones who smelled, what kinky stuff they were into. Most johns are a-holes anyway."

"What do you know about the two victims?"

"Not too much really, but I want to help you find the son of a bitch that did this to them, because what happened to them could happen to me. Are you any good as a detective or are you just another bullshit artist?"

"Let's see what I can do, then you can judge me. Is there anything you can do to help us? Anything you can tell us?"

"I think it was a john that's doing it."

"Why do you say that?"

"Unless it was some crusader that wanted to get us all off the streets, but I got an idea it was some john with a bug up his ass. Most of the johns are weirdos in one way or another anyway. Sickos."

"Did any of you guys work for escort services?"

"Are you kidding? We would never have worked for escort services. They want too big a cut of what we earn. We're all basically street guys. We get some calls from our regulars or we call them, but mostly we work the streets when we don't have johns lined up."

"Are there any other kids you're in contact with?"

"There's really only a few of us street guys left, although I know some guys by sight, guys I see on the streets."

"Is there any chance we can meet and talk, Tim?"

"Yeah, only if it's just you and me. And later, not now."

"That can be arranged."

"Give me your cell number, Delaney."

Denny gave him his number.

"What else can you tell me about the two young men who were killed?"

"Nothing much, except they didn't deserve to die the way they did."

"Do you know where they were from? Where they lived?"

"Sean lived with a john most of the time."

"Where?"

"I don't know for sure. I think in Jersey. Yeah, must have been Jersey. He came into the city on PATH. Used the Christopher Street Station."

"He didn't stay with his john every night?"

"No, sometimes he'd get an overnight with another john. We can't turn them down. Overnights pay well, and you usually get breakfast."

"Do you live in Manhattan?"

"Hey, let's not start getting personal. Unless, of course, you got some hidden agenda, eh? A little bit on the side?"

Denny ignored the innuendo and said, "When can I meet you?"

"I'll let you know."

"You may be in danger. We could offer you protection."

"Yeah, and use me as a decoy."

"No, we wouldn't do that. Anyway, I don't think a decoy would work in a situation like this. Are there any particular johns you think might be involved?"

"No, no one guy that I can think of, but Collie and Sean were scared, I know that."

"Did they share johns?"

"What do you think? How do I know? But maybe not because they were different types. Johns favor certain types. Some like Hispanics, some don't. Some like blacks. You know, dinge queens. Others don't. If you're paying, you have a right to discriminate, don't you?"

"Were they close buddies, Sean and Collie?"

"No, not really. I doubt it. None of us were close friends, just working guys sharing stuff. Like a group of Wall Street guys who get together after work and shoot the shit about stocks down at South Street Seaport."

"Did the johns hang around gay bars?"

"Are you kidding? A lot of johns don't even drink. Some johns don't even consider themselves gay. They really insist they're straight. They have as little to do with gay life as they can. Some of them have fetishes, kinky stuff they're into. One guy just likes to feel thighs, over and over again. Then he jerks off. They are the most screwed-up bunch of losers I know. You get to know what a john likes if you see him often enough.

"Most of them are the dullest people you'd ever want to meet. Real dopey. I swear some of them are the most boring, dumbest people alive. Most hustlers are smarter than the johns they go with. The johns say the same things over and over again. Keep asking you the same questions like they have Alzheimer's. They're like broken records. A-holes!"

"Did any of the hustlers go to particular bars?"

"Like hustler bars?"

"Or bars where you saw johns, met up with them?"

"No, there really aren't any hustler bars like there used to be in the olden days—like when you were a kid. Even the streets nowadays are different, from what I heard. There's a lot less action than there used to be. Port Authority was a big pickup spot, but since way before Nine-Eleven even that place has changed. From what I heard the AIDS thing really cut back on the whole hustler scene. The kids and the johns got spooked."

"No indoor pickup spots?"

"Yeah, maybe Bloomingdales. Especially the men's department. No, but that's gays interconnecting, not a hustling scene. Look, I gotta go. I'll call you later, some other day on your cell."

"Wait. I want to meet up with you."

"Yeah, I'll do that, but not right now. You sound like an okay guy. We might even be able to hit it off together."

Denny laughed to himself, *What is this? A come-on?*

As Denny began to ask another question, he realized the line had gone dead. He opened his laptop and entered as complete a summary of the conversation as he could and saved it in the file folder called *River Homicides*. It was a password-protected file that only he and his team could access. Rich and Terry could read the summary on their laptops and be up to speed on what he had learned, but The Pigmy would never be able to obtain access. Denny wanted to process the information before it slipped out of his hands.

8

One night in the Rum House bar of the Edison Hotel, Denny and Monica were talking. José had just served them. They had just seen a revival of a musical which neither one liked. Monny said, "For me it died onstage. The show didn't know enough to limp offstage and put a bullet through its head."

Denny laughed at her capsule critique. He had a feeling it would appear next day on her blog.

Monny started a conversation with a couple from Cincinnati who had just seen the musical *Chicago* which seemed to Denny like it had been playing forever. The husband went outside for a smoke, and while he was gone the wife told Monny she and her husband had been having some big arguments in the past few days.

Denny thought that if two women felt empathy with one another, there would be little they wouldn't tell each other even at a first meeting. The woman had been drinking, and the liquor was loosening her tongue. Monny was always a sympathetic listener.

While they talked, Denny was reliving in his mind his early days with Monica. They had a stormy relationship for the first two years. Monny didn't quite trust Denny then. He was a good-looking stud that women went after. He had lied to her a couple of times, okay, white lies, but she'd caught him and had become uneasy about him. How much, how far could she trust him?

Their arguments had been titanic. Monny had a tendency to call for a time-out of a week or two, which pissed Denny off more than anything else. One or the other would finally give in and call up the other. But Denny had no patience and got stressed out. He knew they loved each other, but he couldn't predict when she might blow up over some slight.

He was afraid of total commitment at the beginning. Gradually, understanding grew; each became a lot more patient.

Once it got very close to a permanent fissure, but Denny came to realize how much he loved her. She had called a time-out without telephone calls. He walked through a fog when she wasn't around. He got stressed out, couldn't sleep, and realized he was thinking about her twenty-four/seven.

He had no one close to him that he could confide in, to talk about his problems which made it more difficult. Alone, stretched to the breaking point, he called her, and she acted like nothing had happened. They spent one whole afternoon talking, and a lot was settled.

Denny sat nursing a Diet Coke while the two women talked. Her husband must be a chain smoker, thought Denny. A buddy of Denny's, Fred, who worked the investment banking phones at Citibank, sat down and started a conversation.

Denny said, "You guys keep getting your big bonuses even though us poor taxpayers end up bailing you out."

Fred said, "Yeah, I work a seventy-hour week and generate about one hundred million in trades, and they give me a hefty year-end bonus, I'll admit, but I think I earn it. You know the saying in my business, 'We expect to eat what we kill.'"

"Jeez, what a horrible way of putting it."

"It's the truth, and whoever asked you to be a low-paid public servant? I don't make any apology for what I rightfully earn by using my talents. You put a bag of gold in front of anybody, they're going to reach for it."

"You greedy bastards. People are right about those bonuses. They're shameful."

Fred laughed. "Den, think of a bonus like a real estate broker's commission. Very similar. And, Den, let's talk about something else. I don't like having an argument with a guy who carries a piece. It makes me uneasy. I'm always afraid of barfly rage with a cop who's packing. All I have is my Blackberry."

It was Denny's turn to laugh. The husband came back into the bar, and Denny and Monny were soon on their way home.

9

The setting was depressingly familiar, though this time it was an illegal dumpsite along the Harlem River—deserted, desolate like a battlefield. A shroud of clouds covered the sky. Floodlights and a canvas shelter were set up, a light mist chilling the onlookers. The body of a young man, artfully arranged like the remains in a coffin, face upwards, dead eyes staring up at a black clouded sky of nothingness. It was a body carefully, respectfully arranged, the feet together, one hand clasping the other on the chest. Again, a good-looking young man, perhaps Hispanic, with short ebony hair.

Grim-faced, Denny stared down at the body. Another kid cut down. The waste of another human life. He thought of the evil bastard who had committed this atrocity. A shriveled-up soul, black as pitch. To Denny, an unrelenting monster to be destroyed and made to pay.

Denny, leaning over the body, with latex gloves stretched on his hands, pried open the boy's mouth, and with tweezers supplied by Rich, probed and found there the telltale condom wrapped in blue plastic, the talisman. He dropped it into Terry's outstretched evidence bag.

Rather mechanically, without any hope of finding anything, he started his search of the boy's front jeans pockets, jeans so tight that he had to wedge his hand in. The killer always removed every scrap of personal identity. Front pockets—empty—that figured.

He raised the left hip slightly, groped into the left rear pocket. He could feel the boy's buttock under his hand. Zilch. Then he lifted the right hip, probed that pocket. His fingers felt something: flat, smooth, like a thin wallet. He pulled it out. A little address book. He quickly flipped through it. Full of writing in cramped penmanship. This might be their very first lead. Had the murderer left this deliberately, perhaps to send them on a wild-goose chase? There was a good possibility it would be a dry hole because the perp usually was so thorough.

The mist had turned into a persistent rain that began falling in earnest. There was little to do while the forensics team and the coroner's people worked, so Denny, Rich, and Terry hurried back to their black SUV. Rich, in the driver's seat, started the heater and defroster. Terry was on her cell phone in the front passenger seat calling in details. Rich put on the dome light. The windshield wipers were scanning back and forth.

Denny, still gloved, flipped through the book. Names, addresses, telephone numbers, e-mail addresses, lots of them, in a small tight-but-legible handwriting. It might not even be the boy's book. Some had only a first name, some both names, some nicknames, some merely initials. "B.O. Bobby" with a telephone number that said "cell" after it. A medical clinic in the Bronx. "Sis" with an e-mail address. "Anal Al" with an exclamation point. "The Crisco Kid" with a telephone number. The number for a Domino's pizza outlet. One entry said, "Jumbo Jolly, reaming" with a skull and crossbones, but no telephone number. Some crossed-out names and numbers, but with only a single line running through them so they were still legible.

Denny would have to call in more detectives to thoroughly check out this much material. It would take a long time, a great deal of grueling telephone checking and legwork.

Denny continued flipping through the book. When he got to the S's, his heart skipped a beat. There it was, a name he knew all too well—Jake Sigman, a well-known Broadway and film character actor. His father had introduced him to Jake years before when Denny was probably in his early teens. He was a good friend of Denny and his father. Denny and Jake would often trade banter at Sardi's, Joe Allen's, Angus McIndoe's and other Broadway insider theater hangouts. They would kid about Jake's latest Broadway roles.

Jake was a staple on Broadway and was seldom without work. He was fairly famous, always in demand, a solid, reliable actor. When he died, the *Times* would surely give him a good-sized obit. He'd played a wildly campy queen in the British import *The Rice Queen Spy* and had created a lot of buzz in that role.

The mainstay of many a Broadway play, he was never the lead but always had juicy roles that made him a hit with audiences. He was more often than not squiring around some gorgeous showgirl, decades younger than he. Denny and his father had surmised he was bisexual, that he played both sides of the street. There had often been rumors that he was bicoastal, and his beautiful female escorts were beards to cover up his real tastes.

Denny knew that finding Jake's name might be damaging to the actor, and it could well wreck their friendship, but he was on a mission, and a bar friendship wasn't going to deter him from finding a killer.

A few hours later Denny and Rich were standing outside the door of Jake's apartment on Central Park West. Denny hadn't bothered to announce their presence from the lobby and had cautioned the desk attendant not to notify Jake.

Denny pounded on the door and rang the bell. Sigman, in a silk dressing gown, angry and annoyed, opened the door. A startled look appeared as he saw Denny and the large stranger standing there. For several theater beats, he froze. Then the professional actor went into gear. He started playing a role. A smile slowly appeared, but a phony and insincere one. He gave Denny a big show-business hug and looked quizzically at him.

"Denny, babe, what is this, for Christ sake, a raid? Hey, I gave up pot years ago, and I had time to flush my coke down the toilet. To what, my dear friend, do I attribute this unannounced-but-welcome visit? No kidding, what is this? Who is this handsome gentleman accompanying you? What the fuck is up, babe? How's you dear old dad?"

"He's okay, Jake. I'm here on business. This is Sergeant Richard Walters."

Jake shook hands with Rich.

"Well, come in, guys. Welcome to my humble abode."

He led them through an alcove into a spacious living room, the walls full of theater posters. A lot of Sondheim stuff. Big windows that provided a breathtaking view of Central Park. Jake sat in a leather armchair while Denny and Rich perched on the matching couch. Denny pulled out a photo. It was a close-up death photo of the boy's face that had been taken in situ. He handed it across to Jake.

Jake took a pair of glasses from his robe pocket and gazed at the photo. Not even an actor could duplicate the look that came over his face. His features collapsed. He stared. His eyes teared up, real driven genuine tears. This was coming from a man who made a living out of faking emotions but couldn't control his inner self at that moment.

Denny thought Jake was probably in his midseventies. His face, without benefit of make-up or actor's guile, turned ashen. He had neither his public going-out makeup or his stage makeup to mask his age or his shock. He seemed to age perceptibly as Denny and Rich watched his reaction.

He fell back against the pillows of the couch and stared up at the ceiling, breathing heavily. Then he straightened up, and his eyes traveled around the room as if assessing it for the first time.

"Why do we bother to keep on living, to keep hurting ourselves over and over again? He's dead, right?"

Denny nodded.

"Look at what happened to this poor kid. Look at what happens when you try to buy or sell a few hours of happiness. When you think you got life licked, it kicks you in the butt."

He paused, looked down at the floor. Then he addressed Rich, ignoring Denny, "His name is Manuel Guiterrez. Never knew where he lived. I've known him about a year. We saw each other twice a week. Usually for a couple of hours. Each time I paid him two hundred. A few times he stayed over for the night. I really cared for him. I would never have hurt this kid. He was a sweetheart. I think he liked me. Let's not use the word *love*."

When Jake was displaying emotion, it was difficult for Denny to tell which part of this person was on view. Which was the actor, and which was the human being behind the role? Was it role-playing, was he displaying rather than showing true emotion? Was this the real Jake, or Jake the actor, being revealed? With a man who had spent a lifetime on stage, it wasn't always clear where life and artifice began and ended.

When Jake turned to Denny, his look was not friendly.

"Denny, do I need to get a lawyer?"

"I don't know, Jake. What have you done that you might need a lawyer?"

"Nothing. You tell me, buddy. I would never harm this kid nor anyone else. I haven't seen him in well over a week. Denny, is he really dead? I know you wouldn't be here unless he was murdered. But, Denny, I thought we were friends. Why did you come to my home like this? Why did you bring this other officer with you? Why did you have to show up with the cavalry for a friend? My God, I thought you knew me. I love you and your father. Couldn't you have done this some other way?"

"Jake, my hands are tied. Procedures have to be followed, and . . ."

"Fuck procedures, Denny, you shit! What you're doing is unforgivable. You're treating me like a common criminal. Why don't you handcuff me, make me do the perp walk, fingerprint me, photograph me, have me rendered to Egypt, send me to Syria for interrogation?"

"Jake, now you're acting. Cut the bullshit. We have work to do. I need your cooperation, not your Tony award–winning crap. Your name and telephone numbers were found in this boy's address book. He was killed, and his body was dumped like a sack of garbage alongside the river."

Denny didn't want to give away how the victims were "arranged."

Denny went on, "What do you know about this kid? This is serious business. You're not going to need a lawyer if you're up front with us about this."

"Denny, I've known you since you were a snotnose kid tagging along after your dad. You know me. You know I would never hurt any human being."

"Maybe you paid somebody."

"Oh, for God's sake, give me a break. What do you take me for? Why would I kill a kid who never hurt me? A kid who gave me a bit of comfort. What motive would I have?"

"Jake, for your sake, talk."

"Den, I think you and your dad guessed a long time ago I swung both ways. Mainly gay. I paid for sex with guys because I like young guys. Young gays don't want old farts like me. I told you his name was Manuel. I met him one night when I was coming out of a restaurant on Forty-sixth. You know, on Restaurant Row where your dad lived, and where you still live to this day. You probably got his old apartment, probably still rent-controlled, no less. You climbed on your old man's back to get where you are on the cops today. You'd be walking a beat if it hadn't been for your father."

The last cracks really got under Denny's skin, and he was ready with a fierce retort, but Jake plowed on.

"Manuel and I started a conversation that night. I took him home. He proved to be a kid I could trust. We hit it off."

Denny, still irritated, asked, "How did you keep in touch?"

"He'd call me. We'd set up a date. He gave me his cell number, but I only used it a couple of times. He was such a vulnerable kid. A nice kid. He told me all about his lousy family upbringing. As far as I know, he didn't do drugs. He didn't seem to have girlfriends, and he was as gay as a three-dollar bill in bed. He loved to cuddle. I think he thought of me as a father figure. Probably a grandfather. I would never have hurt that kid. I think I loved him."

"What was he like in recent weeks?"

"He seemed scared about something. He talked about the river killings. Said he was afraid of going with johns he didn't know."

"Later, you're going to have to come to the station to make a statement."

"Hey, Denny, I know the drill. I said those same lines dozens of times on the Inspector Frye TV series. But you know what, Dennis? I seem to remember when I played Inspector Frye interviewing a true friend, I'd go alone and I'd make it as unofficial as I could. I wouldn't bring Sergeant Monk with me. That inspector didn't drag his friends down."

"Jake, that was a character on a television show. This is real life. This kid will never breathe again. He'll never see the sun again. There's a big difference between your world of acting and the grimy world we live in."

"But I never thought you'd treat a family friend like shit, and . . ."

"Cut out the fucking bullshit, Jake. Don't try to pin a guilt trip on me. If you know anything, tell me now. I'm not accusing you of anything, but if you know something of value, spit it out now, or next time I'll drag you down to the precinct."

"I know nothing other than what I told you, Mr. Delaney. Now, please get the fuck out of my house, and if you have anything to say to me, call my lawyer. Your dad is a decent human being. You're nothing but a shitass punk who doesn't deserve to live in your father's shadow."

If Jake had been a young man, Denny would have taken a swing at him. He was livid. He turned his back on Jake, and started toward the door. Over his shoulder he told Rich to get Manuel's cell number from Jake. A teed-off Denny charged from the apartment. Out in the hall he tried to cool down while he waited for Rich to come out.

10

Denny got a call from Harley Stennis of Sex Crimes. "Lieutenant Delaney?"

"Hi, Harley. Call me Denny, please."

"Okay. Denny, we may have a lead. There's a well-known john, a big obnoxious fat guy, a slob called Jumbo Jolly, who was seen talking to victim Number Four, Manuel Guiterrez. I know where I can find him. How 'bout we pick him up and bring him in to you for a workover?"

Denny said, "By workover, do you mean the third degree?"

"No, ha, Denny, of course not. I mean interrogation. We only give them the third if they take the Fifth, hey?"

"Yeah, okay. Yeah, bring him in to us. Do you think he might be a live one?"

"Hard to say. I can't really tell. You never know. I only know Jumbo by reputation, and he might or might not be a candidate. I heard he's kind of a loser, but you never can tell who's got the moxie. Denny, as soon as we pull him in, I'll get back to you. But, Denny, I'm just preparing you. The word *loser* sticks to this sucker like a bad smell, and there's every likelihood, knowing him, his BO may even stink up your interview room. Hose him down first, if you can."

"Thanks a lot for small favors. Okay, we'll be expecting him. Don't charge him with anything. Just give him the person-of-interest crap."

Denny remembered that Jumbo Jolly was one of the names in Manuel's address book.

Two days later the man who went by the name of Jumbo Jolly was sitting in an NYPD interview room. Half the name suited him. He was jumbo enough. Big, fat, but only once in a while a kind of half-smile, a grimace appeared. He weighed around 320 and was a part-time bouncer, security guard, limo driver, car-repossessor, short-order cook, and pizza baker. His real name was Frankie Magalucci.

Denny and Rich had been questioning him, and after a time Denny stepped next door to the viewing room where a TV screen and a two-way mirror gave a view of the interview room. From the viewing room Denny and Terry could see Rich in there sitting at a table with his notebook open while Jolly was slumped over in his chair. Denny got a call on his cell phone. It was from Tim.

"Hey, Delaney, I hear you pulled in Jumbo Jolly."

"How the hell did you find that out?"

"Our grapevine. Ever since these killings started, us guys have been keeping in close touch. One of the guys saw Jumbo being picked up. If you cops got him in for the murders, you're a hell of a lot dumber than I thought you were. That fat slob can't even tie his own shoes. Take a look at his shoes. He wears those Velcro tab numbers. There's no one home upstairs. He's as dumb as they make 'em."

"How well do you know him?"

"Too fuckin' well."

"Tim, give me a rundown."

Tim said, "Jumbo always boasted to his tricks about Mafia connections, but the Mafia is too smart to associate itself with such an asshole as that pig. None of the kids believed him, because he drove a shit box of a car and always tried to cheat them out of the money he promised them. He's an overweight john who doesn't drink booze, has zero self-worth, no self-esteem, and has kinky, nasty sex preferences."

It was ironic that Tim had the johns pegged and psychoanalyzed and was probably brighter than most of them were.

Tim was virulent about Jumbo as he said, "He likes to get reamed. Believe me, hustlers aren't into scat or a mean filthy old ass like that. He has to pay extra, a lot of extra for what he wants. I refuse to go with him. How would you like to hook up with a john who threw his dirty fat old ass in your face? There ain't enough money in the world for me to go with that pig, and he knows it. You'll find out for yourself how dumb that a-hole is. Gotta go."

The line went dead.

Detectives had located Jumbo's junky car; it matched Tim's description of a shit box after it had been towed into the forensics garage. On a preliminary search Forensics could find nothing of value in the car. They would impound it and do further tests.

Denny returned to the interview room. Jumbo sweated bullets as he was questioned. He never asked for a lawyer. At first Denny thought they were onto something as they interrogated him. He looked and acted like a guilty man, but Denny also saw in him a gutlessness and lack of conviction. At one point Jumbo broke down sobbing. He had to continually be brought to the toilet to pee.

Later Jumbo said, "Hey guys, I'm flabbergasping for air in here. Can't you open a window?"

Denny looked at Jumbo in an entirely new light and said, "I'm sorry, Jumbo, but there's no window in this room."

Again, Denny left Rich sitting with Jumbo and went back in the viewing room next door where Terry said, "I don't know. Flabbergasping? I just don't get any intensity, let alone smarts out of this guy. The vibes aren't right. He doesn't come across as someone who would have a mission to kill, and he seems like a dumbass loser to me."

Denny said, "I get the same feeling. He's weak. Not enough upstairs to do much planning. He could be involved with someone else with a brain, but I even doubt that. I have the feeling our real guy is an avenger, clever, settling almost a cosmic score. This guy is too nothing to be an avenger. I could be wrong, but I doubt it. I think he'd trip on his own laces if he had any."

Denny had noticed that his sneakers were secured by Velcro straps. Tim was right on target.

Denny added, "I have a feeling this guy would have left forensic evidence in or around the bodies because he's such a klutz."

Madden from homicide came in. He had been checking on their suspect. He wore a rare smile as he said, "Jumbo's no good for two of the nights. His alibis hold up. One of the nights of a body drop he was in Atlantic City driving a limo. Another drop night he was at a poker party in Providence all night. The guy has a record in Massachusetts, but all petty stuff, no violence.

"Cop up in Boston said he's too pathetic to be a serial killer. Guy gets his rocks off on pizza and donuts. People who know him say that even he doesn't realize how much of a loser he really is."

Hours later after more questioning and checking, they had to let him go.

Denny said, "The guy we're looking for is gutsier and smarter than that clod."

Luckily the media had not gotten any word on the questioning of Jumbo Jolly, so no harm had been done except perhaps to Jumbo's self esteem. *If he had any*, thought Denny.

11

Denny was in Joe Allen's munching on the spiced-up cheese-coated oyster crackers they served as a snack. To Denny they had a cheese popcorn taste. He felt like ordering a martini. That was a bad sign, a real bad omen for him. He finally asked Kevin for a vodka martini on the rocks, and he got a puzzled look, but Kevin had been under so much recession bartender stress that he didn't want to challenge him. He knew that Denny lived right down the block a dozen doorways away, and if he ended up getting soused, he could grope his way home.

Denny nursed the drink by ordering a backup glass of ice and kept on diluting the drink in front of him.

One of Denny's showbiz lawyer buddies, Barry Vasco, sat down next to him and, as usual, shared his lawyerly problems with him.

"Den, you know that revival of the straight play *The Killing of Sister George* scheduled for early fall?"

"Yeah, I think I remember."

Denny had no idea what Barry was talking about but did recall a play by that name.

"Well, they backed out. The producers. It's not going through. They pulled it. We'll have trouble finding another booking for that theater, the Cort. The theater isn't in demand, so it's a lose-lose situation for us. It's on the east side of Seventh Avenue, a hard sell for theatergoers anyway. I told Paul that . . ."

Barry prattled on about insider theater stuff that bored Denny, but he nodded politely and continued to transfer ice cubes from the backup glass to his drink.

Then the lawyer said something that got Denny's complete attention.

"You know that hustler killer case you're working on?"

"Sure, of course. Every waking hour, Barry."

"Did you ever think of looking up Big Sid Kleinman for assistance?"

"Who do you mean?"

"Sid is the one who's writing the book on Manhattan hustlers. It's practically the bible about that stuff. He's not only writing the book, he was working on a documentary about them before his health gave out. Sid has interviewed a zillion of them over the years. He's an expert on hustlers."

"Where is he now?"

"Out on Long Island in a nursing home in Hicksville, I think. He's been having serious health problems. He's close to eighty. I heard he's cashing in his chips."

"How do I get in touch with him?"

"I'm technically still his lawyer from when he was doing some agenting."

"You got his address, his telephone number?"

"Not with me, but I can get it for you."

Denny gave Barry his cell number, and the lawyer promised to get in touch with him.

After Denny left Barry at Joe Allen's, he started back the few hundred feet to his apartment stoop. Even on one drink, he felt unsteady. Walking down West Forty-sixth Street was unlike walking down any other street in Manhattan. So many canopies overhanging the sidewalk, so many restaurants. The names of the places didn't always stay the same. Sometimes an Italian one would go under and become a pub or a Thai restaurant.

Almost all of them had bars, were down a few steps from street level. Shills stood outside some of them trying to entice passersby to go in. Browsers stood outside reading posted menus. The street mainly serviced theatergoers. Occasionally some regulars would wait until eight at night when the theater crowd had cleared out, to go in peace to their favorite places. Then the rush would be over. The waiter might say to a regular, "We got slammed tonight."

The next morning, after Barry left a message on his cell,

Denny tracked Sid down to a nursing home in Bethpage on Long Island. Terry drove Denny out to the facility. Sid was overflowing a wheelchair, at least three hundred pounds of flab, when he was pointed out to Denny and Terry. He had to be pulled away from a card game in the common room. They introduced themselves and rolled him into a corner with wide windows overlooking a golf course.

"Shit, you guys always show up at the wrong time. I was ahead by two bucks. What do you two want?"

Denny said, "We're working a case—the hustler homicides—the kids being deposited at river sites. We'd like some information on hustlers."

"Prehistoric or current stuff?"

"Hopefully current info."

"As you can see from this wheelchair, I have a very limited knowledge on what's going down now. I can't get it up anymore, and paying anybody for sex would be a waste of what little dough I have left."

"Sid, just talk and tell us what comes to mind about hustlers."

"There are all kinds of cruising techniques. One scenario goes like this: the hustler waits at a not-too-busy bus stop—on a street or avenue known to have action guys. Ostensibly he's waiting for a bus so cops can't nail him on a loitering charge. He keeps his eyes on the passing traffic in the lane closest to him. A john drives by as slowly as the traffic will allow, his windows down. John spots hustler. Hustler spots john. Eye contact. Maybe a nod or a smile. John drives by again. Hustler is still there. Same lookie-lookie. John passes by.

"Hustler starts walking slowly in the direction of traffic. Probably has a knapsack. John cruises by. Stops about a half block further on. Couple of words like, 'Wanna ride?' Hustler gets in and bingo.

"Or this second scenario. You like this tactical stuff, officers?"

Denny nodded.

"In this one, two or three business guys, hustlers, are standing on a street corner supposedly shooting the breeze, but very carefully watching car traffic. A john drifts by in his car. Same bit, open windows. Makes eye contact with one of the guys. That guy drifts off down the street. On john's next run, he stops beside the hustler who has broken off from the herd. John ropes hustler. A few words pass, and hustler gets in.

"Cops usually aren't going to hassle two or three guys talking 'cause they don't look like street salesmen. Also, hustlers aren't too worried that the john in the car may be a cop because the rent boy waits for the john to make all the moves, do the propositioning.

"Third scenario is an obvious pickup location where guys are known to hang out. Some place, usually at night, where johns cruise by and hustlers hang around. This is the most dangerous for both john and hustler, but hell, these days you cops are too busy tracking down terrorists to bother with this petty shit."

"How about a john walking up to a hustler?" Denny asked.

"Most johns are lazy and wouldn't think of getting out of their chariots and walking to pick up a hustler, and besides, where are they going to park anyway?

"Naturally a john in a car and a kid on the street is a dangerous situation. The john might turn out to be a psychopath, or the hustler might be ready to rip off the john and rob him. If I were looking for a guy what was knocking off hustlers, I'd look for a john who's cruising around in a car. And some of these weirdos drive vans.

"Might be more than one bad guy involved. In San Francisco years ago these two killers waited in a van parked at a corner, a street that ran into Polk Street. They'd talk hustlers into the van. Looked like there was only one guy. Then kid would get in, and second guy would grab the kid from behind. They were famous. Hey, you guys got computers. Look 'em up. Google their asses.

"And none of these guys are really worried about uniformed patrol cars because generally uniformed cops are not interested in sex crimes. Is this of value to you, or am I wasting my time here when I could be making some dough at the card table?"

"No, keep going. This is helpful stuff."

"In my experience, sometimes a john and a hustler will hit it off and have multiple dates. Sometimes a hustler and john strike up a relationship, and the two stick together for a long time, sometimes years. That kind of thing happens especially when there's a shortage of hustlers. It's safer that way for both parties. But a lot of the creeps, johns, I mean, are always looking for fresh meat. It's a matter of numbers. The more, the merrier. Only one-night, really one-hour stands. They seldom go out twice with the same guy."

"Have you ever known Sex Crimes to use decoy hustlers?"

"Listen to this guy. You're a cop, and you're asking me your business? Jeez, you must be really dense. I heard you were a whiz kid, Delaney, but I guess you're just another a-hole."

Denny gave him a jaundiced look which meant, "Watch what you're saying," but instead he said aloud, "We're interested in your input."

Sid continued, "No, no decoys. I think very, very seldom. It's not worth the city's time. So they catch a john. So what? His lawyer cries entrapment. Then maybe the city gets sued for false arrest. The whole thing isn't worth it. Not worth the city's time to have john decoys either. Too much hassle for nothing. A good lawyer can run circles around a crime that's only a misdemeanor."

"Do you know Jake Sigman?"

"The actor. Of course I know him. We used to hang out together. He pays for sex with guys. I know that for a fact."

"What's your take on him?"

"You mean for this serial killer? You gotta be kidding. Biggest pussy cat I've ever known. Harmless. Basically closeted. He couldn't even rattle his own closet. That's why he's always paying and shepherding those starlets and chorines. They're beards.

"What you want to look for is a guy with a Dirty Harry mentality. A guy prone to violence. An avenger. Not a wuss, but a gutsy, tough son of a bitch. Ruthless. Of course, psycho would be part of the mix. Hey, you're looking for a hardnose, not a pantywaist like Jake. He's the nicest, sweetest guy. Look for an evil, rotten prick. The guy you're looking for is a pro at this stuff."

"Any ideas?"

"I been out of action so long, I wouldn't even know where to start."

"But you'd say we're definitely looking for a john?"

"Yeah, a real sick john, a son of a bitch on a mission. Kookie, nutsy.

"Even though I was a john, I'm going to tell you what they really are. I've had a lot of time to think about it since I lost my ability to get it up. Most johns, as a group, are the most irresponsible, immoral, dishonest pieces of shit you'll ever meet. They have no consciences, no sense of right or wrong. They are completely wasted as far as I'm concerned. They're the lowest form of humanity because they treat their sexual partners as objects, guys they have bought and are taking advantage of.

"Never trust them. Always beware of their motives and their lack of human feeling. They swap and trade tricks with each other as if they are exchanging objects, things. They talk about their tricks as if they are dirt. 'Is so-and-so circumcised?' How degrading and nasty can you get? If the tricks are drug addicts, all the better, because they as johns can manipulate and have power over them. They talk a lot about money and how cheap they can get a trick for, like he's a commodity."

Denny said, "Aren't you exaggerating?"

"Hell no. You want me to introduce you to some of them? You get to know them as johns. They're like icebergs in the sense that the one-ninth above the surface seems like a decent normal human being, supposedly a human being, but the eight-ninths lurking below the surface is the john part, the user, the manipulator, the predator. Believe me, a john is nothing but a piece of human waste.

"You guys might be interested in the money aspect of all this hustling racket. You can always divide johns by how much they are willing to pay. There are the cheapskates, the guys who are penny-pinchers, and the high rollers. You even have the guys who try to cheat the kids altogether. In the old days there were the johns who paid ten dollars, some twenty, and so forth. For quite a while the going rate for a decent trick was fifty bucks. It was like a standard fee. There were always kids around who wanted a hundred and up, but the majority could be had for fifty.

"For years I used to hang around the Gayety Theater. That was a stripper theater, upstairs on the second floor. Real steep stairs too. Across from the Marriott, corner of West Forty-sixth and Broadway above Howard Johnson's. Almost all of the working guys in there would ask a couple of hundred and up. No cheapies there. It was almost like a union they had.

"Johns would hang around until the last show and try to jew the guys down to a hundred or even lower. A lot of the dancers came from Montreal. Most of the guys couldn't dance for shit. They were taught a little dance routine, and the klutzes all moved the same way. Guys would have different costumes: a cop, a marine, or some butch outfit.

"A guy would dance there for a week, about five shows a day. They'd do a teaser dance, keep something on, and then come out for a second dance and do a nude bit with a hard-on. Toward the end it cost more than twenty bucks to get in the Gayety. Just a theater with a runway, no booze.

"On Friday and Saturday nights they'd have big shows with sometimes fifteen strippers. In the lounge they'd have a punch bowl of fruit juice and a bowl of stale potato chips. The dancers would hang around the lounge trying to score tricks. Johns and hustlers would exchange phone numbers. Some famous people used to haunt that place. When I first started going there, there wasn't much tipping.

"Then later it became customary for some customers to put tips on the stage. The place always smelled kinda funky. It had security guards watching the crowd to make sure no funny stuff went on. Way, way back, johns and kids would go behind the stage curtains to fool around. Boy, those were the good old days. Word was Madonna went there for kicks. Someone was going to make a Broadway show of the whole scene.

"What kids charge today I have no idea. Couldn't care less. I started to write a book about them old days. You can borrow the manuscript if you want although it won't do you much good because it's so out-of-date. I have a copy in my room.

"Even some cops used to hang around in the old Gayety. Cruise the gay bars, do the drive-bys. Probably not while on duty, of course."

"Who were these cops?"

"How do I know? I just know they were cops 'cause I used to get around plenty. I had a cop buddy used to tell me. He's since passed away."

Denny said, "If you were in our shoes, again what kind of a guy would you be looking for?"

"I'd be gunning for a guy with a bug up his ass. I'd be willing to bet he's gay but refuses to admit it. Some guy on a mission, a guy with a messianic complex. Maybe a married guy who got HIV/AIDS from a hustler and passed it on to his wife, his girlfriend, or his lover.

"I wouldn't be the least bit surprised to learn that your guy is acquainted with these hustlers and vice versa. And I might be looking for a bisexual. Who knows? I ain't a cop, officer. I can't teach you your jobs unless you pay me big bucks. Only kidding. You've got a tough job with this case, and I don't envy you. Hey, guys, I gotta get back to my card game. There's money to be made out there, and you know at my age, you don't buy green bananas anymore."

They left with Sid's thick manuscript, but Denny doubted

that it would do them much good because it was so out-of-date.

Terry said, "Harley Stennis and Sid ought to get together and coauthor the definitive text on hustlers."

"Unfortunately mostly pre-historic stuff rather than what's happening in today's world," replied Denny.

12

When gasoline prices plummeted, it meant nothing to Denny and Monny because they didn't even own a car. A car, living where they did in the city, and working where they did, would be nothing but a nuisance. But food prices were high for them now that Monny was doing so much organic shopping at Whole Foods in the basement of the Time Warner Building at Columbus Circle.

Monny and Denny had bought a Blu-Ray DVD player but didn't have much time to use it with their new flat-screen TV. Denny bought a Disney "Sleeping Beauty" in Blu-Ray to see how the set worked. They watched it together and loved it, like a couple of kids. It looked to them as if it were in 3-D. Other than that viewing, they didn't seem to have time to enjoy their new toy.

One morning Monica was writing in her blog about the way the stock market was tanking. Alan Greenspan, the former Fed chairman, had given a wimpy pathetic mea culpa for his part in the crisis. He couldn't believe that the free market hadn't policed itself. Monny wrote, "Could he be that dumb, that naïve? I doubt it. His statements over the years in Greenspan-speak, gobbledegook, had fooled a lot of people. The guy was and is a horse's ass."

Denny thought she wrote strong stuff, but that's why her blog was so popular. She didn't mince words, and he loved her for it.

Later, Monny was going through some e-mails generated by her blog. One really got her attention. And then alarm set in as she read the message:

Monica Delaney, your husband, the great detective, seems stymied by the hustler murders. I thought he was the world's greatest sleuth. Is he still looking for

connections, correlations, commonalities? What's the matter? Is he losing his mojo? Can't get it up any more? Everyone always said he was a combination of Superman and Sherlock Holmes. Tracked down the terrorist Felix the Cat even while he was a stumbling drunk. (Your hubby, not Felix.) Maybe you better turn him in for a newer model. Used to be hot stuff before he lost it.

Now he's yesterday's news. Old hat. He can't even sniff out clues like the condoms stuffed into those guys' mouths. He should be farmed out to Florida like his old man.

Monica, baby, you and Denny have been haunting that local pizza joint on Ninth Avenue. Don't you ever cook a decent meal at home anymore? Forgotten how to use the stove? You too busy at the blogging keyboard to prepare a nutritious meal? Isn't pizza junk food? I thought you were a health nut. Whole Foods and all that. Whatever happened to broccoli and veggies?

Hey, I hear he's spearing some dame he works with, Terry Somebody. A real looker. You better make him ditch that broad. She could become his new trophy bride. If I was you, I'd wonder what those two are up to. Hey, I got a name for the culprit. Let's call him the Kondom Killer, eh?

As soon as she finished reading it, Monny, badly shaken, called Denny. He promised to get home as soon as possible. While she was waiting for him, she printed out the e-mail.

When he walked into the apartment less than twenty minutes later, Monny showed him the e-mail. She was very upset about the Terry Kerrigan reference but didn't talk about it.

Denny thought at first it was a mean prankster, but then he realized how much inside stuff this guy knew. No one in the media knew about the condoms yet. He hadn't even told

Monny. And how many people would know he worked with Terry?

Later the computer whizzes in the Department checked the sender's e-mail screen name. It was the screen name of a man who had rented a Kinko's computer and had been provided with a Hot Mail convenience screen name. The employees of the store had been questioned but remembered nothing. The Kinko's machines had been impounded, but the techs said tracing the person who wrote the e-mail would be next to impossible.

He could just as well have sent an e-mail from a stolen or found cell phone. A techie friend of Denny's said there were lots of ways a person could send e-mails to Monny's blog without fear of detection.

Later when Denny was looking at the e-mail, the word *commonalities* struck a chord. It was a word that he had used sometime, somewhere. Had it been with his fellow cops? Or had he used it with his media contacts?

From the e-mail's personal digs, he believed someone was keeping an eye on Monny and him, perhaps stalking them. He notified the Department, and for the umpteenth time a police surveillance squad was assigned to keep an eye on them.

After he had gotten nowhere tracking down the e-mail, the case of the hustler killings took over his mind. He wondered again why the bodies were laid out so reverentially. He had a gut feeling, something about the killings suggested inside knowledge and an intimacy between victim and perp. That suggested a john who knew his victims.

Was Monny's e-mail writer the real perp or a climb-aboard nutcase? Something didn't ring true about the whole case. Something smelled fishy, a bad smell. It was a bad smell that wouldn't go away.

Hustlers were like yesterday's news to most people. They were throwaways. They were stale news like old fish that had passed its sell-by date, rancid butter, sour milk that left those telltales islands of slime on the surface of your coffee.

There was a rotten stink to the case that clung, that hovered, that finally stunk up everything in the area. But what could it be?

The next day Rich came into their Lilliputian office. He had to sit on a stool. Some chairs had been removed overnight. He said, "Fazio has the rag on. He's pissed because the perp got in touch with Monny. He's afraid Monny will put it on her blog."

Denny said, "He has nothing to worry about. I'll talk to him. Monny's a cop's wife; she knows what to do. Besides we're both scared shitless that the guy got in touch with her. Gives me one more thing to worry about. Seems as if half my life is spent with security details keeping an eye on both of us."

That afternoon Denny was riding in the car next to Rich. As they passed West Eighty-eighth Street, Denny saw the marking in the road. He yelled to Rich, "Pull over as soon as you can."

When Rich braked and pulled next to a hydrant, Denny stepped out and scurried back to the corner. There it was. The first time he had actually seen one. In large white stenciled letters it read, "Felix is Back!"

Denny studied the stenciled imprint. He was about to take a closer look when a truck honked at him from behind, and he had to jump back out of traffic. What did it mean? Was it a hoax, a joke, a threat, a prank? From what Wexler had told him, he knew it wasn't the work of kids.

On his cell he called Wexler's office. His buddy, Agent Frank Millau, told him that The Ferret was in Washington. *Probably taking the heat for some screwup*, Denny thought. He told Frank what he had seen, and Frank responded:

"Yeah, Denny, it was just called in to us. Thanks for letting us know. We've dispatched a team over there. Hey, we have to get together for lunch one of these days."

Denny agreed and made small talk for a while. Frank was an old friend, a good pal that could be trusted in the Bureau.

When Denny got back to the car, he explained to Rich about the recurring graffiti, what he had been told by The

Ferret. They drove on. One more thing for Denny to be concerned about—a serial killer on the loose, condom talismans, a scary e-mail to Monica, suicide-vest bombers, his dad's cancer, the financial meltdown, the Felix stencils on the streets, a world gone mad. No wonder people drank themselves into a stupor, he thought.

13

When the call came on his cell, Denny had the feeling it might be Tim, and it was. It was his third contact.

"Hey, have you made any progress, or are you just spinning your wheels, twiddling your thumbs, playing with your Johnson? I can just imagine you broadcasting stuff to all your media buddies."

"Take it easy, Tim. I'm on your side. We don't tell the media what we're doing."

"You're the media's darling. That's what I hear. You love publicity. You thrive on it."

"Look, Tim, give me a break. Back off. I've been having a bad week."

"Oh, pity the poor detective. Having a bad week. What the fuck do you think I'm going through out here with that psychopath on the loose?"

"I'm with you. I was just venting. You may know things that can really help us."

"Preppie kids get killed in Central Park, and the cops are all over it. Some hustlers get killed, left to rot on the docks, and the cops say, 'Good, that's one less fag we have to worry about.' We're lower than rat shit. We're expendable to you guys."

"Not to me. When someone, anyone, gets murdered, I consider it my sacred duty to get the guy and either put him away for life or destroy him. That's what I did with Felix. It's a mission, a calling, as far as I'm concerned. A killer has to be destroyed, permanently put out of action."

"Shit, you sound like a fucking avenging angel to me."

"Look, Tim, I need your help."

"Well, here I am, Officer."

"Tell me about condom use with hustlers."

Tim replied, "Some guys pay extra if they don't have to use

a rubber. I refuse altogether. I make them use a condom if it's anal, and also they gotta pay extra, a lot of extra to plunk me. I tell them to double bag it. That means wearing two condoms, one on top of the other, get it, Detective? I ain't anxious to die. Without using a condom, that's called barebacking."

"Okay, thanks for the info, but stop pushing and cooperate. Meet me. I guarantee I'll be alone. I can help you and the rest of the guys stay alive if I get basic information. Talk to me. I can be your savior."

"Yeah, like Jesus."

"Let me see you, meet up with you. Just listen to me. Back off. I'm the pro. I have the resources."

"You guys haven't proved you're pros at anything."

"Meet me in the Village."

"Uh, maybe."

"Okay. Let's do it. Where, Tim?"

"The Tiffany Diner right near Christopher Street."

"I know where it is. How will I know you?"

"I'm the good-looking sexy guy. I'll be wearing a black sweatshirt with a Blood Sweat and Tears logo."

"When?"

The line went dead. If Tim could help, he'd do everything his own way. Denny thought, *He's going to be a hard case. He could be dead by the time I meet him.*

14

Denny was visiting his parents in Fort Lauderdale. He decided to take a walk along the beach. After parking his rental car at the Galleria shopping mall, he crossed the Sunrise drawbridge, went on a few blocks, turned south onto A1A, and began walking along the wave wall on the beach side.

Across the street he saw the shuttered Holiday Inn, passed the wooded Bonnet Estate, then the empty lots where two small mom and pop motels had once stood. Then he passed another shuttered property, the high-rise Howard Johnson hotel. The Atlantic Hotel was the first new building that hove into sight followed by a sprawling newly built but empty and bankrupt Trump property. It looked like it had been constructed from massive Lego blocks.

Then across the street he saw a new Hilton, a W Hotel and the old Sheraton Yankee Trader that had been redone and was now a Westin with a Shula's Steak House on the ground floor.

Opposite the Yankee Trader, a wedding was going to be held on the beach. Two sections of forty folding bridge chairs had been assembled on the sand with an aisle in between leading to an arbor decorated with some fake flowers. A few guests sat on the wall, sweltering in the bright sun and heat while the photographer and a minister chatted, waiting for the wedding couple and other guests to show up.

"To your left," came a cry, and a woman on rollerblades went tearing by pushing a carriage. Two young studs, tattooed beauties, passed him. Denny could hear, "It'll be a long day in hell before I spread sun lotion on some guy's back."

His buddy agreed, "Yeah, man, that's gross. Fairy shit."

Denny had a regular route; he continued south on A1A toward Las Olas Boulevard. He usually made it to St. Bart's coffee shop near the Swimming Hall of Fame where he'd have a Diet Coke and read a discarded newspaper before heading back to his car along his retraced route.

On his walk he saw some of the same people he'd seen years before. Once a confirmed beach person, always a beach habitué. It was like a disease, the beach. If it got in someone's blood, the real beach people never gave it up. He saw the grim youngish guy with a limp, the thin lady in an automated wheelchair, the guy with a parrot on his shoulder (he usually had a towel on the parrot shoulder so the bird shit would land on the cloth rather than his skin), the girl who jogged with a kind of sideways gait, the fat guy who rolled his bike rather than rode it, the show-offy rollerblader who did all sorts of choreographic stunts, and so many more familiar beach denizens.

That day he had a limited time so he only walked as far as the pedestrian bridge near the Westin before turning back. Before going back, he saw the black conning tower of a submarine in the channel leading to Port Everglades. A Goodyear blimp moseyed along above in the sky.

Denny decided to take a break and sat on the wave wall. Something was bugging him about the case of the slain hustlers. It was like doing the Sunday *Times* crossword. You left it for a couple of hours, and something would pop into your head. What aspect of the case was bugging him? He thought for a few minutes, and then decided that it was the e-mail to Monny. He took out his IPhone and called Terry. He asked her if she had access to the computer case file.

"Yup. I'm sitting right here in front of my computer surfing for porn."

"Yeah, okay, very funny. Would you see if you can find the e-mail to Monny and forward it to my IPhone?"

"Sure."

"Okay, I'll wait on it and contact you later."

Very soon the e-mail arrived. He opened it and started to read the text. Okay, it had a lot of inside knowledge about the case, personal stuff about him and Monny. That wasn't what was bothering him. He was just about to read it for a second time when he heard a familiar voice. It was Don, the Philly bartender, from The Old Florida Seafood House.

"Denny, I thought you were here to exercise. I didn't know you'd be sitting here playing with your IPhone. How do you like it by the way? I am still amazed by what mine can do."

The two chatted for a time. Denny lost his train of thought, but something was still bugging him. He'd continue his walk and look at the message later.

As Denny walked back toward the Galleria shopping mall parking garage along Northeast 26th Avenue, he heard cawing and shrieking. Then he felt something graze the back of his head. He was being strafed. He had walked under a palm tree where some crows had nested. Another one tried to dive-bomb him. They came up from behind, out of his sight line. He took off his baseball cap and looked up where some crows were positioned on a utility wire. One zoomed in again, in for the kill. He waved his cap wildly as he backed toward the garage entrance. One dove from one direction and another from his other side. They were cawing and making an awful racket trying to scare him away.

A family of five, walking on the sidewalk, were approaching him, laughing as they saw him wildly twirling his cap in circles above his head. Denny made sure not to turn his back on the crows. He had heard that birds never forgot the person who had invaded their territory. Once again a crow flew in to get him as he ran into the garage. He looked out, and saw the father in the family of five swatting them away.

The guy yelled, "Wow, these things are friggin dangerous. No wonder that guy was trying to bat them away."

When he got back to the car, he drove off and stopped at Whole Foods to pick up lactose-free milk and OJ for the house. He also bought a copy of *The Times*. He'd read the Arts section first thing, do the crossword puzzle, and then go on to the main section.

Later he told his mother about the incident with the crows.

Carole said, "Certain kinds of birds can be very aggressive."

Denny said, "Thank God our docile city pigeons would never do that. They're too mild, but crows are natural predators."

"Den, it's like your job pursuing human predators. Remember our backyard cat, Toby, actually a neighbor's cat. He haunted our backyard for restaurant leftovers. Where else was he going to get lobster? He was always being dive-bombed by mockingbirds. He had probably gotten into their nest, and they never forgave him for it. A mockingbird would swoop down and dive-bomb him every time he was in the open. They never forgot him, and the poor cat was a victim for life.

"One time he got on his back, and your dad was dumb enough to scratch his tummy. Toby reached out with his paws and pulled your dad's hand to his mouth to give him a love bite which turned out to be a little too much of a real bite. Your father got so pissed off I think he almost kicked the poor cat into the pool, but Toby forgave him. Who else was going to feed him lobster?"

When Denny and Monny visited his parents, Eamon and Carole, the four of them were like first-time tourists. They roamed up and down posh Las Olas Boulevard looking in the shops and sidewalk cafés where they gawked at the diners, and the diners gawked back at them. They'd take a ride out to the huge discount mall, Sawgrass Mills, on the edge of the Everglades, with its hundreds of stores, most of them national chains.

They'd go up to the sprawling flea market on Sunrise Boulevard and cruise among the many stalls. They missed the old days when it had a free circus with elephants.

About once a year they'd take one of the airboats that would transport them into the rivers of grass in the Everglades with its alligators, rare crocodiles, egrets, herons, all sorts of long-legged wading birds, and exotic snakes such as the Burmese pythons that had thrived there even though they weren't indigenous. The reptiles had been abandoned by bored or broke pet owners.

South Beach in Miami Beach with its art deco buildings was an attraction, although it meant driving down I95 with its wild drivers who crisscrossed in and out of lanes and sped with abandon.

A trip on the *Jungle Queen* up and down the Intracoastal and up the New River gave them a chance to see all of the impressive homes owned by celebrities. The narrator gave a who's who list of the top names in show business and industry who had either once-owned or currently owned waterfront homes. The sightseeing boat would go way up the river and stop at a little phony Indian village where a man wrestled some alligators. They were always surprised at the number and size of the iguanas they saw in the yards along the river.

There was plenty for them to do in the "Venice of the Americas" even though it often meant a repetition of what they had seen and experienced previously.

If the weather was warm, they'd swim in the large backyard pool or have a cookout where Eamon presided over his gas grille.

On Saturday or Sunday in the winter season, they might drive over the high Seventeenth Street Causeway to scope out the cruise ships that were in town and stop at Kelly's Landing to get fresh New England fish, fried clams with the bellies and homemade Boston baked beans in a crock.

Late one afternoon while Denny and Eamon were seated on the screened-in porch, Denny was admiring the seven potted desert rose bushes that were in full bloom.

"Dad, you've had great luck with those flowers."

"Yeah, they're great. No watering. Just the occasional infestation of aphids on the blooms or an invasion of those yellow caterpillars. They are the greatest self-sufficient plants for this climate."

"The yard looks great."

"Denny, how's that serial-killer case working out? Someone dropping off those unfortunate kids, apparently hustlers along the waterfront. Any leads yet?"

"No, nothing so far. This guy is thorough. He removes all ID and leaves no forensic evidence as far as we can tell."

"Are they hustlers or not?"

"We think they're hustlers."

"Why does he have a bug up his ass about hustlers? Does he feel wronged by them or something?"

"Don't know. The thinking seems to be that he's a john—someone who knows the score and can pick them out."

"Serial-killer investigations are torturous. It's hard to get a hook on the killer. Is Madden still in homicide?"

"Yeah, he's hanging in there. Keeps him busy since his wife died. A good guy. Sharp."

"You can count on him. As honest as the day is long. A straight shooter. He's persistent. Knows all the angles. I'm glad to hear he's still active."

"He's working his end of the case in Central Homicide."

"Good. Is the FBI involved?"

"Not up to this point. They have a lot of terrorism stuff on their plate in New York."

"Yeah, they'll get in when it looks like a slam dunk. Do you still see that guy you used to call The Ferret?"

"Oh sure, Wexler. He met with me in the Polish Tea Room the other day. He keeps me up to date on stuff they're working on."

"How I loved the Polish Tea Room for their corned beef hash. Jeez, those were the good old days. All that comfort food. The bagels with cream cheese, the matzo soup, those huge muffins. But, Denny, watch out for people like The Ferret. Keep your eyes open. Watch your back and be careful. They love to pass the buck.

"Threading your way through the departmental politics and the FBI's machinations can be daunting sometimes. In the old days when I was in the VIP security detail, it was the Secret Service I had to keep my eye on. Some of those dickheads could be real bastards."

"Don't I know it."

"Department climbers used me as a rung to get up the

ladder sometimes. Denny, when Carole's not looking, would you fix me a Dewar's on the rocks? She can play mother superior sometimes. Don't skimp on the scotch, Jocko."

"Sure, Dad."

"Good lad. She rations my intake, and sometimes I feel like it's Prohibition all over again with her. Den, give my love to all the guys in the bars around Times Square. Tell them I'll be up there for a visit soon. I sure miss that action, the give-and-take of the old days."

Later that night Wexler called Denny's cell while he was at his parents' house. He sounded concerned about something.

"Denny, I know you're at the family's house in Fort Lauderdale, and I hate to bother you. Would it be possible for you to come over and meet me in Naples?"

"Why Naples?"

"Well, I'm spending some time with my family over here. And my mom is sick so I wonder if you could come over here and talk. I'd rather not talk in the New York field office or on my phone if I can help it. Something has come up. I know it's inconvenient, but I'd appreciate it."

Naples was about a two-hour ride across Alligator Alley, now I75, on the west coast of Florida opposite Lauderdale.

"Look, Wexler, I'll talk to Monny, and see if she and I can make a night of it. Would the day after tomorrow, Wednesday, be okay?"

"Yeah, great."

"I'll get back to you in less than an hour."

Denny talked to Monny, and she liked the idea of visiting Naples for a night. They could do some sightseeing and shopping. He was back on the phone to Wexler giving him the heads-up.

Wexler said, "I'll meet you in Tin City."

"Huh? What did you say?"

"Tin City, the shopping place in Naples."

It suddenly dawned on Denny the place Wexler was talking about.

"For God's sake, why there?"

"Because . . . well, it can seem like a casual conversation at a place like that."

Wednesday Denny and Monny were staying at the Bayfront Inn in Naples, a hotel with a marina right across from Tin City. He'd been given directions to get there by his father. His parents knew Naples very well because they went over there frequently for weekend getaways.

Tin City, a group of buildings with metal roofs, a mall housing restaurants and touristy shops, was across the waterway from the inn. The desk clerk told Denny about a shortcut to get there, so while Monny went shopping on Fifth Avenue, Denny took the walkway underneath the Highway 41 bridge and was there in a few minutes.

Denny sat at a high cocktail table at the Riverwalk Fish & Ale House. A waitress approached, and he ordered a Diet Coke. When it came, he sipped and waited. He watched a pelican swoop down low over the water. Small pleasure boats plied up and down the waterway. He waited for twenty minutes. He had the feeling that someone was checking him out, seeing if he was alone.

Wexler walked in, all garbed up like a Floridian with khaki shorts, a tee shirt, and sandals. He sat down across from Denny and ordered a gin and tonic. After the waitress left, he started talking in his low, conspiratorial voice.

"The Grand Central guy, the vest bomber, was interrogated."

"With waterboarding and sleep deprivation?"

"Cut it out, Den. Yeah, we pulled out all his fingernails, and then gave electric shocks to his balls. Of course not. Sometimes you bleeding-heart liberals get everything wrong. He was only too willing to talk. He was completely cooperative. He claims he was acting alone, no accomplices, no cell, no network. Nada."

"How did he learn how to make an explosive vest? Wouldn't that take some help? Where did he get the explosives?"

"He claims he learned all of the details from the Internet.

He showed us the sites and went through the process step by step. Most of it seemed to fit. We can't be absolutely sure he wasn't coached to give us this Web site information. He claimed he stole the explosives over a period of time from his uncle who is in mining out West. We found out his uncle *is* in the business and he says, yes, he is missing some explosives. We learned that the nephew, the would-be bomber, did have access when he worked for the uncle."

"So, everything gels?"

"No, not really. In some ways it seems too pat."

"What was the guy's motivation?"

"So far, he says grievances and injustices. A lot of unspecified stuff."

"Was this guy trained in a camp?"

"As far as we know the guy has never left the states. No foreign contacts. Seems as if he's never gone to any training camp anywhere in the world."

"So, what's up with this guy?"

"That's where the whole story gets loose. He doesn't make sense. It sounds too contrived, too easy. This is where you come in. Denny, he's heard of you. Knows all about Felix and your interrogation of him. He's read the book that Len Harrington wrote. He desperately wants to talk to you. In fact, he says he has to talk to you. You specifically. Could you interview this guy for us? Why not give it a shot?"

"How can I say no, but what makes you think I'll get any more out of him than your guys did?"

"We're going by what he says. He's got the hots about talking to you and you alone."

"Oh, great."

Denny told Wexler that as soon as they had set up a time, he'd try to make it. They talked for a while about approaches and techniques, and then Wexler said he had to leave to see his mother who was having a bad time of it in a Naples nursing home.

After Wexler left, Denny stared out at the pier and harbor. On the dock was a pelican with a piece of plastic meant for a six-pack draped around his neck. With his foot he was trying to free himself from it.

15

It was the November weekend after Barack Obama had been elected president. The financial crisis was still in full swing, Wall Street was tanking except for an occasional rally day. Unemployment was 6.5%. General Motors and Chrysler were in dire straits, running out of cash.

More than half the country was jubilant about Obama's win, but it would be until January 20th that he would take over.

People on Wall Street were more worried about keeping their jobs than going to Christmas parties, but they were still hoping to get fat year-end bonuses. The owners of restaurants and theater producers in midtown were worried that the spillover from the crisis would really start hurting their business.

Denny couldn't remember a time when so many Broadway shows had decided to close early in January. Theaters were offering all sorts of discounts to lure people in. Sandwich-board people meandered up and down Times Square advertising the farce "The 39 Steps" and offering discount tickets to most shows. You could see gloom and doom on the faces of people scurrying to and from work. Despair was contagious.

NYPD Manhattan Homicide had a weekly summary of pending cases. Denny noticed that the hustler killings were getting a low priority. Denny thought, *Hustlers are expendable. Until the case is built up as a serious serial-killer event, the Department and the media will give it short shrift.*

He thought of making some calls to his media contacts to stir things up, but then decided that he'd better wait. The brass would know he was the source and get pissed off. Better not to rock the boat at this stage. His day to use his media contacts would come.

Denny loved Michael Connelly's crime novels. In the books

Harry Bosch, the L.A. detective, was always on a mission, driven by inner demons to speak for the murder victims, the dead. He was an avenger. He was always at odds with his bosses, and his love life was perpetually a mess. Come to think of it, Harry was a mess, a mournful soul. He was his own worst enemy. Connelly had other protagonists, but he seemed to always return to Harry, as if he couldn't get Harry out of his system.

Denny liked Connelly's complex plots, the way he created mazes within mazes and kept the readers guessing. Harry had a hate-hate relationship with the FBI. Denny felt for Harry because he was often in Harry's shoes as far as the FBI was concerned.

There was usually a time in a Michael Connelly crime novel when his Harry Bosch studied the murder books. Denny had piled up the homicide bureau's murder books for the slain boys. Denny thought the ones he was examining were thin compared to many case books he had seen.

Each murder book had photographs of the crime scene, of the body in situ, and it cross-indexed the videos that had been taken. It had forensic reports, lab tests, the medical examiner's file, the pathologist's autopsy report, interviews by investigators, summaries by detectives, timelines, phone tips from the hotline, anything and everything related to the homicide. The NYPD insisted that no preliminary conclusions, assumptions, or theories be included, in case the books ended up in court.

Denny knew there had to be a thread of commonality running through these cases other than the river discovery locations, the strangulations, and the wrapped condoms in the mouth.

He thought of how infrequently male hustlers were written about or featured in the media. There was little public interest in them. They ceased to be news unless some bigwig was caught fooling around with a rent boy. Or they popped up briefly in the news when they ended up as the end product of some serial killer.

Who would really care about them, with so many other things in the world to worry about? The only people who would possibly care would be their families, if they knew, other hustlers, and, oh yes, cops like him who made it a mission to find the murderers. And perhaps people who were paid to take an interest like crime reporters.

Even the DA's office had little interest in them when they were alive, because they considered hustlers of legal age engaging in consensual sex with johns, practically victimless crimes.

Denny went through the books again. Had a hustler given someone HIV/AIDS? Was it a moral crusade to rid New York of sinners?

Hustlers made easy prey because they'd get in a vehicle or go with almost anyone who offered them money. Could women be ruled out as perpetrators? He'd heard some of the hustlers carried switchblades to protect themselves.

He looked at the days of the week, times of the month on which the murders had been committed. No clue there.

He wondered: why the river drop-off points? Perhaps because New York has miles of waterfront, and usually the highways running parallel to the waterways provide easy access to river locations; but was there something more to it? Why were the corpses laid out so circumspectly? Respect? Because there had been personal contact? Perhaps because the killer knew his prey. Maybe they were ritualistic, sacrificial killings?

16

That Wednesday after Thanksgiving, Denny and Monny were talking about the terrorist attack on Mumbai. Years before, they had taken a cruise with Denny's parents aboard the *Global Quest,* which ended up in Mumbai overnight. They had spent the night there aboard ship before the four of them disembarked and took a flight to New Delhi. From there they had taken a long eye-opening bus trip to Agra to see the Taj Mahal.

Denny said, "I can't believe it. How could ten guys wreak such havoc? Killing almost two hundred people? Apparently they came ashore in a small boat. They struck a lot of the places we visited on our trip—the Leopold Café, the central train station, the beautiful Taj Hotel, the Oberoi Hotel. Remember those great places?"

Monny replied, "Sure I do, but where were the police, security forces during all this mayhem?"

"Looks as if the places weren't guarded with enough security of the right type. The element of surprise. But if they had armed guards in sufficient numbers, this thing might have been minimized. Just in normal times, you'd think the number of armed police and security guards would have stopped some of them, but when they holed up in the hotels with hostages and grenades, they were a bitch to stop."

"Could it happen here in the states?"

"Sure, they could choose any number of targets. It's a wake-up call for us too. We have to make advance plans for such attacks. We need armed people, not just in uniform, not just at entrance sites, but also stationed like snipers within sight of entry points so they can pick off incoming attackers. Armed guards at the entrances to places are going to be the first targets. We need marksmen out of sight, ready to take down intruders. The grenades this bunch used made the whole thing more dangerous too."

"I wonder," Monny asked, "how safe my Smith Barney building really is even with its own security people."

"With an attack like this, not that safe at all. I've been thinking back to when Felix planted his bombs at Grand Central. If a suicide gunman had attacked, there would have been a lot of armed cops, National Guard, and other security people, but with Felix and his planted bombs, the element of surprise was devastating.

"One thing these places need are a lot more armed nonuniformed people, guards in civies who aren't immediate targets. If the attackers had shot up the guards at the doorways, they couldn't have gotten in and wandered around causing a massacre if plainclothes security guys had also been on duty. They should have had armed guards in mufti."

"Shouldn't the police, the FBI, and private security be rethinking all of their plans?"

"Of course. One answer is pre-positioning security in spots where they aren't initial targets. All these cops at entrances are to make the public feel secure, but we need unseen security more than the visible ones. In hotels and office buildings, you can't let them get beyond the lobbies. The Taj Hotel on the upper floors was a real maze and a shooting gallery that offered plenty of evasive places for gunmen to hole up."

"When guys are suicidal, can you really prevent them from acting?"

"Only by stopping them as fast as you can. And entry by a small boat is another thing that can be impossible to prevent. God, what a mess. These guys were suicidal, yes—but pure evil sociopaths, and clever planners."

"Then this thing where a cruise ship almost gets captured by pirates off Kenya. Luckily it finally outran the pirates."

"Hey, hon, no one ever told us we were living in a safe Utopian world here. This is a goddamn dangerous place we're living in."

He wished he could tell Monny about the suicide bomber

who had almost wreaked havoc at Grand Central Station, but that would really rattle her cage, thought Denny. *It sure as hell rattled mine.*

Monny said, "Your serial killer? Why would a guy want to kill hustlers?"

"Mon, that's what we're trying to figure out."

"Punishment, retaliation, retribution, for kicks, just because they're there and easy to get at? To stir the pot, because the killer is a psychopath, a sociopath, some type of assorted nutcase? Or maybe because everything has become freaked out in life today?"

"Boy, hon, you really have thought all this out."

"Den, I'm looking at your case from a distance. Maybe you're too close to it. Move yourself out into space and look at it vertically instead of horizontally. Do some lateral thinking."

"Jeez, Mon, I'm glad you and The Pigmy never connected."

17

This time Hal Madden was driving Denny to the crime site in a homicide-division unmarked Crown Victoria. It was a little past dawn so there was plenty of light. North of the Triborough Bridge past the East 138th Street bridge, Madden turned onto a street with old industrial buildings. They headed down a lane that led to the Harlem River.

They passed a dilapidated factory building with a drainpipe that was spewing a sickly yellow stream of waste, possibly toxic chemicals, emptying into a small creek that probably found its way into the river. Madden pulled up behind a group of assorted police and other responder vehicles. Denny recognized his squad's black SUV. They walked to the yellow crime-scene tapes. A uniformed officer lifted the tape so they could duck under. The ground was wet and muddy.

Captain Fazio, aka The Pigmy, greeted Denny. "It looks like another one. This would be Number Five by my count. The media is going to be all over this. Keep me apprised of any and all developments. I'm going to the office and see if I can help coordinate a press response."

"Yes sir. Will do."

Denny thought, *He wouldn't be any help here anyway. Probably getting his elevator shoes all muddied up.*

As Denny approached the body, he was greeted by Terry and Rich. Terry said, "It looks like we've snagged another one. As soon as Otis and the camera guys get through, we can take a closer look. Forensics has done quite a bit already."

Dr. Otis Lanning, the old veteran assistant medical examiner, was kneeling next to the corpse humming to himself as he often did when he was examining a body. He looked up and saw Denny.

"Top of the morning, Lieutenant Delaney. Looks like we're in for a nice day, judging by the sun. Your subject here is very much like the others. Looks like he's been deceased for about twelve hours. Just a guesstimate, you understand. Also, I would probably wager that the foul play had occurred elsewhere. You're keeping me awfully busy with your river cases."

Denny could see that the body, as before, had been laid out and arranged in a proper display.

Lanning said, "Where's your guy with an evidence bag?"

Rich, preparing for one of Lanning's disapproving onslaughts, held open a plastic bag for Lanning. The doctor reached his gloved hand in the mouth of the body and drew out a wrapped condom which he deposited in the bag.

"Denny, your killer is going to deplete the city's condom supply. You better nab him before we run out of rubbers."

Otis creakily rose, expelling a flatulent chirp, to a standing position. "We'll know more when we get him on a table."

"Otis, does it look like a strangulation?"

"Yes, but I think this was a face-to-face encounter. Looks like he might have been throttled head-on. Take a look at the guy's arms. There's bruising as if he had to be held in place."

"Doesn't that suggest more than one person? One holding him, the other doing the strangling?"

"Can't say because the bruising might not have been contemporaneous with the strangling. You're the one getting the detective's pay, so you're going to have to figure that one out. How's Pops by the way?"

"Seems to be holding his own so far. Has the cancer at bay."

"Good, give him my love. Tell him a little scotch won't hurt him and may even help."

Otis spotted Terry. "Oh, and little lady, I didn't see you standing there. Pretty as ever. I hope you're not letting your skin dry out. Always use a good moisturizer, honey. Try to use an ointment, not a lotion; it'll work longer."

He patted Terry on the arm as he made his slow and

stately exit from the scene like an old-hand, hammy actor exiting the stage after playing Lear.

Denny stared down at the victim. Young, early twenties, good-looking, thin, with a look of surprise on his face. The victim's clothes were wet from a recent rain. Garbed in latex gloves, Denny knelt down and went through the pockets of the body. After a few minutes of searching, he said, "Nothing here."

"Terry, when they post the situ pictures on the computer, send them to Sex Crimes and see if they can ID the victim. I don't suppose there were any witnesses?"

Rich answered, "None that we've been able to find. Detectives are fanning out through the area seeing if there might be a security guard, a dog walker, or whatever. It's not a place where anybody lives. That's why the killer picked this spot for the body drop."

Denny looked at the damp ground around the body and then at the soles of the victim's sneakers. "No sign of mud or any of this local ground area muck. Looks as if he was carried here. Was the ground around here pretty well tracked when you guys got here?"

"Yeah," Rich said, "Forensics said it looked like an army had tramped through here. It rained a couple of hours ago so this mud might not have been here when the body was dropped off, but the lab guys said it would be impossible to isolate footprints because it's such a mess."

Denny said, "I want to get his in situ face photos to the media as soon as possible so we can get an ID and maybe stir up some tipsters. Let's look around this area and see if we can find anything."

A TV crew had pulled up not too far from the yellow-tape area. Uniformed cops were making them move further up the lane.

"The hyenas are circling," said Terry.

Denny said, "Before we're through, we may need these hyenas to stir things up and get the public more involved and alert. We need witnesses to these drops."

18

Denny was on the phone to Lieutenant Marco.

"Lieutenant, I wonder if I could meet with Stennis and Slattery and get a general idea of what kind of cases they usually run."

"Sure, Delaney, anything that I can do to help. You know how anxious I am to cooperate with you. All you have to do is ask. When would be a good time for you to huddle with them?"

Denny could hear the sarcasm in Marco's voice and the territorial whine.

"How 'bout this afternoon?"

"Okay with me."

"I'll have them here at two. That copacetic with you?"

"Great, see you."

When he got there, Marco, sensing an impending territorial incursion, sat in on the meeting. This time it was held in a large airy room with a large oak table and comfortable arm chairs. Denny addressed the two sergeants while a somber, wary Marco looked on, his neck as usual spilling over his too-tight collar. Slattery didn't smile, was only minimally polite, while Stennis was the good old boy, loquacious and outgoing as usual.

Denny began with, "Guys, what I'd like to get is an idea of what a typical case in Sex Crimes might be like. Maybe typical is the wrong word. Let's just say a sample case."

Stennis laughed and said, "Your timing is perfect. We're just winding down on a case now. This may take a little time in the telling, so be patient."

Slattery added, "Yeah, Stennis can be quite expansive if called upon."

Denny said, "I'll be tolerant. Fine, take your time, Stennis."

"Here's how it went down. A man named Thomas Stiles, a guy with a lot of money—we're talking millions here—he's semi-retired, now a so-called consultant. Sold some patents to a big chemical company and made a fortune. Travels all the time. A john. Likes kids, I'd say from seventeen to midtwenties. Right, Jerry?"

Jerry merely nodded assent.

"In the late eighties this guy buys a condo unit in a converted brownstone on West Forty-eighth between Eighth and Ninth. You know the neighborhood, don't you?"

Denny agreed, but sensed that Stennis knew he lived on West Forty-sixth, Restaurant Row, two blocks away from the street he had mentioned.

Stennis continued, "Now this Stiles gets a terrific buy on this place. It's nothing special. A studio. The guy has a cot and a couple pieces of thrift-store junk furniture. Pure junk. Crap. Orange crates would be upscale for this piker. He's always traveling. Florida, Prague, Vancouver, Chicago, all over, you name it. This place on Forty-eighth was a, whatta you call it, a pied-à-terre. How's that vocabulary for a dumbass sergeant?"

Denny replied, "Great."

"This pied-à-terre he'd use when he'd spend a couple of weeks cruising around looking for kids while he's in Manhattan. Does the same thing all over the world. I'd call him an obsessive screwball. A pure unadulterated, certifiable ding-a-ling. Cheap as shit. Eats crap. Basically a miser except he has little places all over the world that he owns because he's too cheap to pay hotel rent. Get the picture?"

"Kinda. Sounds sort of unique to me."

Slattery contributed for the first time by saying, "We got a lot of info from Stiles's fellow johns."

Stennis continued, "Johns who were only too happy to report negative stuff on this a-hole. Before I give you the guy's whole life story, let's cut to the chase. About three years ago, this weirdo meets a kid named Tommy Stasio in Central Park. Kid at that time was twenty years old. Stiles brings the kid back to his place. Stiles admits they had sex. After having sex, they have a big argument."

Stennis had a short coughing spell, but then took up the narrative again. "It took us quite a while to break down Stiles to find out what the quarrel was about. Stiles had agreed to pay the kid forty bucks. Afterwards Stiles says he was only going to give him twenty because the kid wasn't worth it. We're talking about a guy with millions here, but also a stupid fuck. They argue, fight. A major disagreement. The kid grabs a hammer and cracks it into the side of Stiles's head. Stiles passes out. Lot of blood, of course. Don't ever try to sucker a trick after you've agreed on a price. Dumb move.

"An acquaintance of Stiles—and I emphasize acquaintance 'cause this creep Stiles has no real friends, I would bet, anywhere on this planet. This acquaintance has a date with Stiles for eight o'clock that night. This whole sex thing went down in the afternoon.

"Acquaintance bangs on door, can't get in. Stiles had given this guy a key in case of emergencies. Guy comes in the apartment, finds Stiles bloodied, unconscious. Calls Nine-one-one. Medics take Stiles to hospital. He has a bad wound and concussion. They keep Stiles in the hospital for five days. A-hole still has a scar on the side of his head."

Marco hadn't said a word. He probably knew the whole scenario anyway, and might even have told Slattery and Stennis to tell Denny about the case because it was such a long-winded story that Denny might tire of the narrative halfway through. Stennis took a swallow of water from a bottle on the table and resumed the story at that point.

"This is where we entered the picture. Stiles come to our cop shop and reports the whole thing. He's actively looking for this kid because he wants him prosecuted. At that time he had no name for the kid. He gives us a description that could fit a million kids in New York. He wants vengeance. He says he'll find him personally and notify us as to the kid's whereabouts. This guy is a cheapskate on a mission. Even with his millions, he'll stop at nothing to catch this fuck.

"Meanwhile Stiles continues his travels all over the world to God knows where. Probably Thailand, Vietnam, Prague, Burma, the Philippines, wherever there are cheap tricks to be had. He's in and out of New York, maybe every couple of months. Well, one day he spots the kid in a pizza joint on Ninth Avenue not too far from his own pad. He follows the kid to a tenement near Port Authority. Calls us up. Gives us the address. We go there and stake the place out.

"Remember this Stiles is a wealthy bastard, and you never know if he's pushing some buttons to get action from higher-ups in the Department, so we have to be proactive. We spot a kid coming out of the building, a kid that fits Stiles's general description. We collar the kid. Bring him in, and Stiles identifies him. Kid gets locked up. No bail.

"Later, much later, the case goes to court. Kid gets five to seven on assault and attempted homicide counts. Coulda been worse, but the kid's lawyer brings up soliciting and gay stuff. Says Stiles forced drugs on his client, etcetera, etcetera. Still later Stiles sells his Hell's Kitchen property and, as we far as we know, doesn't come back to the city because he'd have to pay for a hotel room. Says he never liked the cruising in the city anyway."

Denny asked, "Any chance he could be our river killer?"

Slattery and Stennis both said no at the same time, but Stennis asserted, "We got to know this guy pretty good in all that time. He was always checking in with us, bugging us about catching the kid. He's vindictive, but he's not the kind who would be a crusader after a whole mess of kids. Nuts in his own way, but I don't see him as a serial killer and besides, as far as we know, he's never shown up in New York again. Basically not a guy who'd use violence himself. A coward. An asshole worried too much about his own liability."

Slattery said, "I have to agree with Harley. You get to know a guy when you see him often enough. I just don't get the feeling that he would run a campaign like your guy is doing. He told his friends he likes to cuddle with the kids. This guy is a pussycat who may like cuddling except he's too pathologically cheap to pay for or invest in a relationship."

Denny left soon after they'd finished. The case they had recounted didn't seem to help him much, and he got the feeling it wasn't meant to. He'd be willing to bet the two sergeants and the lieutenant would be glorying in the fact they had stonewalled the famous detective. What they didn't know is that they had whetted Denny's appetite for more information.

19

Denny was sitting in the Tiffany Diner on West Fourth Street not far from Sheraton Square. He had taken a booth in the half-empty restaurant, and in order not to make the waitress unhappy, he ordered a BLT club with french fries and a diet Coke. He had brought along a prop book so he'd at least look busy with something. The twenty-four-hour place was a favorite of all sorts of Villagers and particularly popular with the gay and lesbian population.

He was early, but he hoped that Tim would scope him out and see he was alone. He had come on the subway from Times Square. He sat waiting, glancing at his Connelly mystery but not really reading it. After a long wait, a young man with a Blood, Sweat and Tears sweatshirt entered and looked around. Denny nodded, and Tim came over and sat down in the booth with him.

He was clean-cut, early to midtwenties, handsome, neatly dressed, a guy with Calvin jeans, thin but with a good body. He was preppie looking. Short blond hair, about five foot ten, light brown eyes. Denny could imagine him being in demand. He had a boyish look, but also a mature attitude. He offered his hand. They shook hands—Tim had a firm grip, not wimpy or off-putting.

"I recognize you from your pictures, officer. I'm Tim, as you probably guessed. I haven't sent a proxy."

"Tim, call me Denny. It makes it easier."

"Okay, Denny. So you're the world-famous detective who brought down Felix the Cat. If things were more normal, I'd like to have a chat with you about your cases, but nothing is normal or ordinary anymore. Someone out there thinks us kids are prey, and he is hunting us. If I can be of any help at all, that's what I want."

"I think you can be a big help by giving us background

information. You were certainly right about Jumbo Jolly. He turned out to be a real loser."

"You'd think your guys in Vice would have known what an a-hole he was. Any fool could figure out how dumb that piece of shit was."

The waitress came to the table.

"What are you going to have, sonny?"

"Exactly the same thing as my dad."

The waitress looked at him, and huffed as if she didn't believe the "dad" stuff, but she wrote down the order and walked away.

Denny laughed. "Thanks, Son."

Tim said, "Look, I have some theories."

"Okay, try them out on me."

"This is a knowledgeable guy you're looking for. Someone who knows the drill. Street hustling in Manhattan is like a closed corporation. It isn't as open as it was years ago. Johns have to know where to go and who's who. This may sound stupid, but the guy you're looking for may have been a hustler himself at one time. Now he's twisted, round the bend."

"Anything else?"

"The guy is clever. No dope. I don't think he acts on impulse. I think he plans out this stuff, knows who he's looking for and where to find him. He's vengeful, a nasty piece of work. You gotta catch him."

"You think he's targeting specific guys?"

"Yeah, I think so. Guys he's met or guys he knows by sight or knows through other hustlers."

"Do you think this could be a john who is accompanied by a hustler?"

"No, that doesn't make sense to me. Of course, I don't know for sure, but I don't think a young guy would be acting like a scout because he could end up the next one to go. And I don't think a young guy would turn on his own kind. Your guy thinks things out. He's clever. Knows the scene, and he's a calculating son of a bitch."

"Any more theories?"

"I think it's a guy rather than a woman. I don't think a woman would get involved in something like this."

"No, we don't think it's a woman either, but we can't rule out anybody."

They talked for a considerable time, but Tim didn't seem to have any definite information.

Denny asked, "Did you ever see any of the victims with specific johns?"

"No, I can't say that I did. I pay attention to what I'm doing, and I don't get involved with other guys very much."

Eventually Tim said, "Look, I gotta get going. If I get any dope on anything related to the case, I'll get in touch with you. Incidentally, you're a very good-looking, sexy guy. I just wanted to say that. I know you're straight, but you are a hunk, my type."

"Thanks for that, I guess."

"Look, Denny, let me get outta here. Give me about fifteen minutes before you take off, okay?"

"Sure."

"Nice meeting you. How 'bout I grab the check?"

"No, it's on me, Son."

"Thanks, Dad."

Tim walked out quickly. Denny wrote some notes in his notebook to kill time and to give Tim a chance to clear out of the neighborhood.

20

Denny was about to interrogate the vest bomber. When Denny entered the room, he could see that the suspect was a nervous wreck. His hands were shaking, and he was sweating so much his face was drenched with perspiration. He smelled like urine, and he had more facial tics than a psychologist would be able to count. Denny introduced himself. He regretted shaking hands with the poor bastard because the guy's hands were so clammy. When the guy wasn't looking, Denny wiped his hands on his jeans.

The young man said, "Hello, my name is David, but you probably know all that already. You're the Felix detective. The guy that executed him."

This guy is already annoying, thought Denny.

"Well, it wasn't exactly an execution, David. When someone is trying to kill me, I have a tendency to defend myself. But let's just have a little talk here. Please try to relax and calm down as much as possible. You have nothing to fear from me. I just want to have a quiet conversation."

"I'm a mess. I peed in my pants. I can't hold it. I'm afraid I'm going to shit in my pants too. I hardly eat whatever it is they give me. I can't sleep. They won't give me anything to help me get a night's rest. I can't function. I just want to die."

"David, don't say that. There's always hope. I think I can help you."

"I hope so. I asked for you. I need to talk to you."

"I want you to relax. I'll see if I can get something to help you sleep. Some Ambien maybe. Now let's just talk. Tell me anything you want to about what happened, what led up to your troubles. I'm here to listen, to help you."

"Really?"

"Yes, believe me."

"It was about injustice, about inequities."

"Who was being unjust?"

"People."

"Which people?"

"Do you think if I had some nice cold water that it would make me pee all over myself?"

"Would you like me to get you some ice water?"

"Not right now. I bet you're thinking this guy is looney tunes, off his rocker."

"I'm not judging or making assumptions. I just want to listen. I'm here to help, David."

"You're working on a serial-killer case now, aren't you?"

"Yes, but that has nothing to do with this conversation. I work temporary duty for the FBI, and I'm here in that capacity."

"Who do you think is killing those young boys?"

"That's what our police department investigation is trying to learn. Right now, interviewing you, I'm helping out the FBI."

"Do you ever wonder why we're here? What life is all about? What God's intent is for us?"

"Sure I do. Everyone does. Why did you make a vest bomb?"

"To stir things up. Make people think. Make them see the inequities, the injustice."

"Don't you think that's kinda general. Could you be more specific? Are you a Muslim or a sympathizer of certain extremist Islamic movements?"

"No, of course not."

"Are you sympathetic to Palestinians for example?"

"Who do you think is killing those kids whose bodies are found along the river?"

"Hey, Dave, let's stick to your problem. Not mine. That case has nothing to do with you, okay?"

"But I'm interested in your life. Your new case, the one you're working on now. I've read your book."

"Oh, you mean my friend Len Harrington's book about me and Felix, *Nine Lives, Two Men*. He was the reporter who wrote the book. He was murdered by Felix. It wasn't my book."

"Yes, Felix the Cat. But the book was about you. I've read it six times."

Denny was growing apprehensive. He sensed trouble. This guy seemed to be going off the reservation, straying in the wrong direction.

Denny said, "Why so many times? What was the great appeal of that book for you?"

"When I did what I did, with the vest bomb and all, I wanted to be Felix the Cat all over again. Then I chickened out, because I really didn't want to hurt people, to kill innocent people."

"Why would you want to be Felix? He was a murderous, evil bastard."

"Yeah, but he had a goal in life. According to your book he was speaking for and fighting for the Palestinians."

"Again, not my book. A hell of a way to speak for someone. He wasn't fighting either. He was basically a coward, certainly not a suicide bomber. He was a terrorist, terrorizing. That's a different ball game from fighting in combat, putting your life on the line. He was a gutless bastard. And do you think the people he killed, their friends, lovers, family, knew he was doing it for the Palestinians? To them it was just senseless killing. Random slaughter."

"But he had a mission in life."

"Yeah, he was a killing machine. Did you get your inspiration or whatever motivated you from that book?"

"Yes, sorta."

"That doesn't make me feel very good about myself or the book. I never thought the book would be a bad influence on people. It's like a kick in the gut for me to hear that. I never would have agreed to the book if I thought it would have a bad influence on people."

"So, do you think you'll get a book out of this serial-killer case?"

"After what you just told me, I hope not. No, I'll guarantee you. There will absolutely be no book from this bad dream I'm going through right now."

"Could I have that water now?"

Denny noticed David was calmer, more confident, almost cocky.

"Yeah, sure. I'll order up the water."

Denny went to the phone and asked for the water. The whole interrogation was being videotaped and observed anyway so he wasn't telling those on the outside what they didn't already know.

While they were waiting for the water, David sat there silently. Denny couldn't think of a way of reinvigorating the interrogation to get any real information out of the guy. And besides, he felt devastated by what David had told him. David had a playful grin on his face as if he had just conned someone.

God, was the guy gloating? Denny wondered.

When an agent brought in the water, David drank it down and said, "Mr. Delaney, I'm tired now. I don't want to talk anymore, okay? I want to go back to my cell and rest."

Denny stood up and shook hands with him. It was useless to go on, and Denny felt miserable about some of the things David had said. Perhaps on another day he'd be more forthcoming. Denny didn't know whether he had broken the ice or fallen through it.

21

Denny was coming out of one of the courtrooms downtown when he happened to see Sergeant Slattery in the corridor. He was a guy who intrigued Denny because when he and Stennis were together, Stennis always had the podium.

Denny said, "Jerry, I wonder if I could talk to you for a minute?"

"Well, Lieutenant, I've really gotta run, and I don't have much time. I'm on a tight time schedule."

"Hey, Jerry, I'm on a tight time schedule as well. It'll only take a minute. I just want to ask you a few things."

"I . . ."

"No, come on over here for just a minute. Slattery, this case has priority over everything else."

Denny led him to an alcove bench where a lot of sunlight was flooding in. They sat facing each other. Slattery was always well dressed, didn't have that rumpled look that some cops had. His button-down Oxford shirt was starched and spiffy. Everything was very tasteful about his dress and was suggestive of money. Slattery reluctantly sat down.

In the glare of the sunlight those translucent blue eyes were startling. Dark eyes seemed to point inward and were seldom the outstanding feature of a person, but truly blue eyes fascinated a dark-eyed onlooker, and were sometimes striking and absorbing.

Slattery was a very handsome man, but his brow was furrowed. His face was not that of a happy, contented man or one who was comfortable in his own skin. Perhaps these killings were taking their toll on his psyche. He kept staring down at his hands, off into space, anywhere but into Denny's eyes. But when he did look at him directly, Slattery's eyes were hypnotic because of their vivid blueness.

"Jerry, I wanted to ask your opinion on some things. Where do you see this case going? We seem to have hit a big snag, a dry hole. Everything has come to a stop. Usually Stennis gives me background, but I want to hear from you what you think is going on."

"Well, Stennis is an expert on the gay life, the hustlers, the johns, what makes them tick. To tell you the truth, I was never that involved in homicide cases, and it's hard for me to suggest approaches. I feel sorry for the kids, but if someone unknown to us is going after them, we all just have to hope for a lucky break. You know more than I do how this whole thing works. I heard you were even trained at the FBI center at Quantico."

"Yeah, that's right, but it doesn't make me a seer. What do you think of the theory of johns being controllers, control freaks?"

"Yes, Lieutenant, I think johns are control freaks. Why they became johns is one story, but once they are there, they want to be in charge. They're the ones paying for it after all. Why shouldn't they get what they want?

"They're the bosses. They want the kid to do what they want, what they are told to do. After all, the hustler is being paid; he's the subjugated one, isn't he? He's not the boss. In a manner of speaking, he's the slave, and the john is the master. But it's more subtle than that for the john and the hustler. There's a game going on. And sometimes rules are being made up as the game goes on.

"Neither party has a rulebook, but they know there are rules, and the rules have to be obeyed. If the rules aren't followed, there are serious consequences."

Denny asked, "Aren't there cases where a shrewd trick manipulates his john and runs the show?"

"Yeah, I suppose so. Hey, there are no easy answers. This is human psychology we're dealing with. Sometimes it may seem as if the hustler is in control. It's complex. It's not an easy thing to figure out, and nobody has the answers, even a psychologist or psychiatrist. Stennis and I have both attended seminars on human sexual behavior as part of our training.

"Sex is never easy, never simplistic. It's always complicated and multilayered. There's always so much going on below the surface just as in a heterosexual relationship, a marriage or a partnership. The guy you want to talk to is Stennis. He's the expert on john-hustler relationships."

"No, Slattery, I'm a little bit tired of listening solely to Stennis. I want to hear what you have to say. Don't pretend to me that he's the brains of your team. He may be the old tried-and-true veteran, but don't play dumbo with me."

Slattery said, "You can be in this business all your life, and you'll never figure it out. And, you know what? As human beings we're not meant to ever figure it out. Only God can do that. Hey, look, Lieutenant, I really gotta get going. I wish you all the best on this, and Stennis and I are working twenty-four/seven to help you."

He got up and scurried away. Denny had never heard the man talk so long before. He'd have to get him alone again, away from Stennis, to learn more. Separated from Stennis, he had a lot to say.

22

Denny called Wexler.

"What's the latest on the vest bomber at Grand Central?"

"Could you come down here to see me? I'd rather explain in person and not talk on the phone."

"Okay. When are you free?"

"How about right now?"

"Okay. I'll be there. About a half hour, all right?"

"Sure, Den."

Denny noticed that he had gone back to being summoned to Wexler's office. Had he been downgraded again by Wexler? For some reason cabs were hard to get, so it took more time than usual to get there.

When he got to the FBI field office, Wexler had him sit next to him on a couch in his office. In the old days Wexler always had to have a desk between them. Denny thought, *Boy, this guy is really changing. Maybe I should start calling him Bruce.*

Wexler said, "I've got some bad news. A couple of nights ago, David was having very bad anxiety attacks and was physically in bad shape. He was rushed to the hospital."

"Oh, on the way to the hospital he escaped like Felix. Another FBI screwup."

"No, Denny, it's something much worse than that. Yesterday he passed away."

"Passed away? Just like that? What was the cause of death?"

"We are trying to determine that right now. It appears to have been a heart attack, but other conditions might have been involved. The guy had a number of things wrong with him."

"It wasn't a suicide?"

"No, though he hadn't been eating or sleeping."

"But there must have been an exact diagnosis of the cause of death. He was a young man, for Christ sake."

"The medical people are working on it. They think it was a massive heart attack. An autopsy is being held."

"I feel terrible about this."

"So do we. What he gave us up to the point of his passing wasn't really satisfactory."

"One thing really distresses me: the idea that this guy may have been motivated by the story of my pursuit of Felix, and Len's book which detailed what happened. That really shook me up."

"The guy was unhinged, Denny. He was a loose cannon, was unbalanced. We'll never know the full story of what made him tick."

"Isn't it awfully convenient for you guys that this guy just passes from the scene, dies, goes off into the sunset with none of the big questions ever answered."

"Stop with the conspiracy theories, the blame-placing game. We're all on the same side in the war against terrorism."

"Do you really take yourself seriously when you use that expression 'the war against terrorism,' or are you practicing for some public pronouncement? You sound like Bush and Blair, for Christ sake."

"Den, as far as the public is concerned, this guy never existed, he never tried to blow himself up in Grand Central. He never surfaced in the media."

"There were rumors."

"Rumors, but no facts. Remember, you knew nothing about this guy. We agreed on that."

"Yeah, of course I agreed, and I'll never be a source. Do you want me to sign a confidentiality agreement or something? But the poor guy did exist, and he did almost create mayhem. For what real reason I don't know."

"And neither do we. Denny, let it go. He's gone. It's over. Like a lot of other things, nothing ever happened."

"Did you ever notice in recent American history how often

nothing ever happens in life? No one ever disappeared in renditions. No one was ever tortured or waterboarded. Weapons of mass destruction were never found. Osama bin Laden disappears and can't be found. We just go on. Well, I've got a serial killer actively on the loose. Let's hope he shuffles off too."

"We'll be glad to assist you on that case. But, Denny, as long as we've known each other we've been dueling with each other about the government's policies."

"Agent Wexler, that's for damn sure."

23

This time it was a parking lot next to a small channel of the Harlem River. Again the body, Number Six, a young man's, was laid out decorously, respectfully, on display for mourners. Once more there was a wrapped condom stuffed in the mouth of the victim.

It was early morning with the sun up. Denny, Terry, and Rich were getting to the scene about six hours after it had been discovered. The medical examiner had been delayed. One of the first detectives on the scene was Denny's friend, Hal Madden.

He approached Denny and said, "Den, we may have hit a bit of luck on this one. I put on my gloves and lifted the boy's shirt. Under that polo shirt, he's wearing a tee shirt. Something caught my eye. Near the hem of the tee is a little sticker with NYSDC followed by a long series of numbers. I've seen that before. It's a New York State Department of Corrections laundry code number. They keep those numbers on their twenty-four-hour data base. I went back to my car and keyed in the number on my laptop for the NYSDC data base. And bingo."

"Great work, Hal, but we gotta consider that this kid might have found or been given the shirt."

"Oh no, Den, I realize that. I'm calling it a possible ID. Name is Thomas Stasio."

"Wait a sec. That name rings a bell."

He turned to Terry and Rich. "Guys, does that name mean anything to you?"

Both said they couldn't recall hearing the name before.

Denny said, "Somewhere, in some connection I've heard that name."

Denny walked over to the edge of the parking lot. He flipped through his notebook. Nothing. He thought over the various files that he'd read. Still nothing. He was about to return to the group huddled around the body when it popped into his brain. He walked back to the group.

"Listen, it came to me. Remember when I attended a meeting with Stennis and Slattery on my own, and they described one of their routine cases to me? The case involved a kid with this name, but he's still doing time. Was sentenced to five to seven, and he couldn't be out on the street so soon."

Madden interrupted him. "No, the data base says he was let out on parole. He didn't even serve his minimum sentence. How and why that happened I don't know. Maybe he benefited from a budget cutback."

Denny turned to Terry, "Please try to get either Slattery or Stennis to hightail it over here as fast as possible. I want them to ID this guy."

Terry had to make several calls in order to get through to Sex Crimes and get her message through.

Denny said, "This is too much of a coincidence that this kid gets hit. I think Stennis and Slattery have to go back and look at the john that was involved. A guy named Stiles. This kid was targeted I'm sure. Maybe that vengeful john got to him. Maybe this is a copycat killing."

Terry said, "But, Denny, the condoms, the way the bodies were laid out never got in the media."

"The condoms, no, but photos of the dead kids have appeared in the media. And maybe the condom stuff has leaked out."

It took an hour for Stennis to get there.

Stennis looked down at the boy.

"That's him. I saw him enough times in court."

"Do you think your john on a mission could have done it?"

"That guy, Stiles? We'll check, but as far as I know this guy is somewhere in the world chasing cheap tricks. He doesn't seem the type, but you never know. Believe me, we'll find the fuck. Does this victim fit your killer's MO? If our guy did this, it means he did all the others. He could have flipped. Let me make some calls to his so-called friends. They'll know where he is."

24

Rich said, "Hey, Denny, look at this article in *The Post*. This may have something to do with our case."

Denny took the paper and read the story. It was by Denny's pain-in-the-ass columnist nemesis, Packy Pucker.

GRAY PREDATOR NABBED

Shortly after one thirty a.m. on Wednesday morning, an elderly man stumbled into the emergency room of St. Vincent's Hospital, badly bruised and cut, shaken up, with a black eye. The man, identified as Jerome Franklin, aged 81, had a harrowing tale to tell. He had been sexually molested, raped, by a man marginally younger than himself. Mr. Franklin reported that he had met the alleged rapist in the County Squire Club, an upscale gay piano bar, a so-called "wrinkle room" or "elephant's graveyard" where older men congregate to meet men who are similar in age, mostly late fifties, sixties, seventies, and up. Older gay men who are attracted to other older gay men.

The Manhattan Sex Crimes Unit was called in. Detectives Jerry Slattery and Harley Stennis of Sex Crimes spent several days questioning patrons of the gay establishment which occupies three floors of a townhouse in the East sixties of Manhattan. After investigating, the detectives secured a warrant for the arrest of Mitchell D. Fenton, age 68, who was alleged to be the perpetrator of the crime.

Several patrons of the Country Squire Club reported that Fenton had on different occasions accompanied elderly men to their residences where he reportedly abused and raped them. He was fairly well known in the bar, and witnesses said that victims were afraid to report the crimes to the police for fear of retaliation or because of embarrassment. Some patrons no longer frequented the bar because they were apprehensive about running into the alleged gray-haired predator.

It is alleged that he only preyed on older men, never on younger men. His preference was for men his own age or older. He was very intimidating, one customer reported. The management of the establishment claimed that they had never received a single complaint about him and said that if they had, they would have permanently barred him from the establishment.

One patron alleged that Fenton had accompanied him to the patron's home where Fenton proceeded to rape him. The older man, the victim, protested vigorously, but Fenton, a large muscular man, forced the victim to comply.

Fenton was booked, and police are seeking additional victims to come forward and press charges. As a result of the investigation, already four victims, all elderly men, have appeared and accused the alleged attacker. Some months ago one man confronted Fenton in the bar and was warned by Fenton that there would be serious consequences if he reported an incident of sexual assault. The man left the bar and did not return. His friends who still frequented the bar alerted him, and he, too, has now filed charges.

Fenton at his preliminary hearing told this reporter, "I'm not denying that sexual encounters took place with older gentlemen, but all sexual contacts were consensual, and, as you can see, all of my supposed partners were certainly of legal age when the

alleged sex took place. These are old men looking for attention. They are pathetic creatures. If I assaulted them, why didn't they turn me in? All lies. All of it. Fabrications by losers. These old geezers are all pitiful liars."

Denny said to Rich, "Please, go on the computer and get me the docket details on this bust. Everything they have."

A few minutes later, Rich said, "Denny, this is interesting. The docket lists the arresting officers as Stennis and Slattery, but also lists Detective, junior grade, George Timmons of the Sex Crimes unit. Who the hell is he? Have we ever heard of him?"

Denny got on the phone to Lieutenant Marco.

"Lieutenant, on a docket report we read the name of George Timmons of Sex Crimes. How come we never met this guy or knew about him? Is he in your unit?"

Marco's tone was decidedly cold and indignant.

"Lieutenant Delaney, I thought we all agreed to keep our eye on the ball here. Timmons is just back on duty. He has been on disability leave for six months. What he has to do with your case is beyond me."

"I still should have known about him. I want to see this guy and talk to him."

"Hey, he's out of the loop. What the hell are you trying to stir up here? Why don't you concentrate on your homicide cases? I never saw a publicity hound that did the Department any good in the long run."

"Wait a sec. I want to schedule a meeting with you and Commander Foxe to get some things settled. If you're running a rogue outfit there, I want to know and get this all out in the open."

"Look, Lieutenant Delaney, I'll schedule a meeting between you and Timmons this afternoon. Does that satisfy you?"

"Fine, Lieutenant Marco, but you insult me again or impede my investigation in any way, you'll wish you were walking a beat on Staten Island."

After meeting times were settled, Denny hung up.

He turned to Rich and said, "Cripes, I really know how to ruffle feathers, but the guy has got a hard-on about his unit. He's too defensive. It's not just loyalty to his own men. I sense something creepier than that, but I think I've made a permanent enemy out of that jerk."

Later that day Denny, Terry, and Rich sat down with Timmons in the Sex Crimes squad room. Lieutenant Marco was nowhere in sight. Timmons was having trouble with his back. They could tell he was in pain. They talked about the collar of the gray predator, and Denny questioned Timmons about his work in Sex Crimes.

Denny asked, "How often do you team up with Stennis and Slattery?"

"Oh, not very often. Ninety percent of the time I'd get paired with some detective drawn from the general roster. Those two, Slattery and Stennis, they always work together. They've been a team for years. You know what it's like on the force with your partner. It's like a marriage. You and your partner might be together for years. You even begin to like the same foods.

"They're very territorial, Stennis and Slattery. Always heads down over their personal laptops. To tell you the truth, they are too tight. It's hard for me to work my cases and get them to cooperate. I've tried to keep out of their way. I've been feeling very uneasy about them for a long time."

"You don't think they're on the take, do you?"

"No, I doubt that. I don't mean that at all. When I started on this squad a few years ago, I could tell I'd always be considered an outsider in their minds. They seldom shared information with me."

"Did you know any of the slain kids?"

"No. That's part of what I mean. They know who's who, and I never got to know much at all. They dealt more with the gay scene than I did."

"What, if anything, did you think they were up to?"

"I don't know. Honestly, it got so I didn't give a shit as long as I was able to do my job. I'm thinking of going on permanent disability to get free of these guys, or at least get a transfer."

"Did you ever talk to Lieutenant Marco about them?"

"Yeah, but he was evasive and gave me the fish eye. Said he was pleased with my work and to forget those bozos."

"And . . ."

"Nothing came of it. Those two guys are experts at compartmentalizing. Male hustlers and johns are their territory, not mine. I might as well be working in a luncheonette for all they care. Share? They don't even know what that word means. They live in a separate world from me.

"I'm moving on, and I don't give a shit about this outfit. Either I'll be on permanent disability or working somewhere else. Who gives a shit? Everything sucks anyway as far as I'm concerned."

On the way back to their office, Denny said, "I wonder if there any more Sex Crimes officers out there that we haven't heard about?"

Terry said, "I'll check with Personnel."

"Yeah, it would be good to find out now rather than learn later."

25

Stennis was on the phone.

"Lieutenant Delaney, some good news and some bad news, depending upon what you're looking for. Stiles, the guy that drove us nuts for years. He's out of the picture. Six months ago he had a stroke while he was in Prague. He's nothing but a vegetable, probably a cabbage, maybe even a turnip, in a nursing home in Pensacola. He can't even get out of bed. Wearing diapers and a catheter. He's been out of circulation for at least six months. A basket case, the a-hole. I checked with the cops in Pensacola and with the nursing home. He's a goner so you can forget about him."

"Could it have been one of Stiles's buddies?"

"Are you kidding? They couldn't care less about him. A selfish, self-centered prick. He doesn't have a friend in the world."

"What was Stasio like?"

"A hell of a lot better human being than Stiles, but a nonentity."

"Thanks, Stennis. Let me know if you pick up anything on Stasio's friends or his johns."

"Will do, Lieutenant. Keep the faith."

Denny told Terry and Rich about the call, and said, "Well, I really never had Stiles as a serious suspect anyway. Another shot in the dark. But why is it, Stasio's name turns up, and then he morphs into a victim? This case has legs. It has a life of its own. As if something gets set in motion, and then the shit hits the fan. It's like self-generating. Don't ask for x because y will happen. Every time I take a step, make a move, something else clicks into the picture. I'm afraid to move because I fear something bad will pop up. Like with Felix the Cat. I'd make a move and that SOB would be making his next pounce."

26

One Thursday Monny had taken a day off from her job, and Denny was not due in the office until late. They were mesmerized by the TV images of the rescue taking place on the nearby Hudson River. The pilot of a US Air jet had made a near-perfect emergency landing on the river after its two engines had been hit by bird strikes as it took off from LaGuardia.

Passengers lined the wings of the floating plane as a flotilla of ferries, excursion boats, and rescue boats took them aboard. The water was icy cold. The drama played out, and the couple watched as New York became the scene of yet another heart-stopping event—this time a near-tragedy. Luckily no one died in the emergency landing.

When the plane was coming in low over the city, many New Yorkers feared a repeat of the Nine-Eleven terrorist attack. The city seemed to always be in the spotlight and the crosshairs. Denny knew some of the river rescuers, and he thought of the killing grounds, the way the shores and piers of the rivers had become the disposal sites for the river murderer.

Denny left for work in the afternoon. Seated in front of her laptop in the bedroom, Monny brought up the latest e-mails from her blog. What she saw frightened her. It was another message from her nemesis:

> **Monica Delaney, do you recall our last visit? Do you remember me? I labeled that serial killer the Kondom Killer? The hustler murders case? I hear your hubby is stumbling and fumbling around trying to find connections, correlations, commonalities. Seems like a bright guy on the surface. Fordham degree, but he's still basically dense. You know that residual alcohol in his system from his days as a lush. You never really get that shit out of your**

system. Those Irish genes, carrying denseness and alcoholism. It clouds the brain. He's still walking around in an alcoholic stupor.

Your guy rides to glory because he's the one who aced Felix the Cat. Felix was an easy target on the stage of a movie house.

He didn't apprehend him. He executed him. That's Denny's style. Prosecutor, jury, judge and executioner—all rolled up into one neat package. Felix never was allowed to go to trial. He might even have been another invention of the FBI. How does anyone really know?

I hear your husband found a victim's address book, and it yielded clues. Maybe he'll get lucky and find fingerprints on it.

Is Teresa Kerrigan behaving herself when Denny's out of your sight? Bye bye, Dollface.

Monnie was furious. *How come they can't track down this guy who is blatantly using e-mails.* She called Denny, but this time her temper erupted, "You've got to stop this shit. He's killing me, Den. The son of a bitch knows everything. He's stalking us. Where the hell are your computer geeks? Catch this fucker and kill him for me."

Denny hurried to Monny after reporting it. As he walked out of Central Homicide on his way to the cab, he kept glancing behind him. The e-mails had made both of them furious and squirrelly. Someone was invading their private space.

This murderer was sending e-mails to Monny—maybe. Or it could be an insider who was a troublemaker. The writer knew intimate details about his life and about the case. Whoever it was, the person knew way too much. The fact that the writer knew details about his life with Monny bugged him more than anything else. When a killer got into your private space, he was very dangerous. He could potentially get at either Monny or himself and harm them. It could be a he or a she, he kept reminding himself.

27

Denny and Monny were in one of their favorite dives, The Bubble Bath Pub on Ninth Avenue. It had scores of neon beer signs all over the walls, a linoleum floor that had been around probably since World War II, and an ancient jukebox that played 45s. It had a long oak bar the length of the room and offered thirty brands of beer and ale on tap. The tiny kitchen turned out some of the best burgers in the city, and its recipe for carmelized onions was so secret that the owner, eighty-three-year-old Bubbles, claimed she would take the secret ingredients to her grave.

Next to them at the bar was a couple who called themselves Bonny and Clyde. Denny thought that they were just drinking buddies. He was draft Sam Adams, and she was rum and coke. Monny heard Clyde talking about something called the death pool. She asked, "What's the death pool anyway? I never heard of it. Maybe it's something I can write about in my blog."

Bonny said, "Well, guys, it's like this. There's seventy-five individuals or couples. We call them teams. What we do is bet on which celebrity is going to croak first during a given month. Clyde and I go in it as a team. We each put up twenty-five bucks. Now, Wally there, our esteemed bartender, he's a high roller and puts up fifty bucks by himself, so he's a one-man team."

Clyde said, "Now this month Bonny and I have Angela Lansbury and Imelda Marcos. All seventy-five teams get two names, so altogether there are one hundred fifty celebs on the list. This is a local death pool made up of people from about four or five bars with assorted relatives and friends. There are probably thousands of death pools all over the world. You can Google "Death Pool" and you'll get about five million hits."

When he heard what they were talking about, Wally came

over to join the conversation. "This month I have James Garner and Carol Channing. The VIPs on the list have to be over eighty to get on. If I win by myself, I'll win three thousand bucks. Paddy Shea over there, Johnny Walker red on the rocks, runs this pool and does the research and collects the money so he gets seven hundred fifty bucks as an administration fee. The pool is over for the month when the first celebrity kicks the bucket."

Monny asked, "Do you have to get both names to win?"

Wally continued, "You only have to get one of your two names. You don't choose the names. They're assigned to you, and if the pool is over for that month, you get two new names. If none of the celebs pass in a certain month, the money rolls over, and you pay for the new month, but you keep the same two names. There's a waiting list to get into our death pool. Bubbles hates it 'cause she's past eighty, but she keeps her mouth shut because it's good for business. Last month I had Jerry Stiller and Pete Seeger."

Monny said, "Oh, God, this is too ghoulish to think about—betting on whether famous people are going to die. I can't believe you guys would do that."

Bonny defended the pool by saying, "What the hell, it's just like betting on the ponies. What's the big deal? It gives little folks like us some fun and suspense, and we all gotta go sometime anyway, so somebody might as well profit from it. It can give us a few extra bucks, and who is it hurting?"

Monny said, "But you guys are sitting around waiting and maybe wishing and praying that your celebrity will pass, and you'll profit from it."

"Oh, Monny, get a life. Don't be such a spoil sport," laughed Clyde.

Wally gave Denny a copy of that month's list. It had the first names or nicknames of the bettors and below each team were the names of two famous people with their dates of birth. Stubby, for example, had Lauren Bacall, 09-16-24, and Burt Bacharach, 05-12-28. He looked down the list. He knew quite a few of the bettors from local gin mills.

Then he did a double take. Near the bottom of the third column it said, "Jerry & Harley." Underneath their names he read, "George Bush, 06-12-24, and Arnold Palmer, 09-10-29." This had to be Stennis and Slattery. The name Harley was too unique, and then to have it paired with Jerry was just too much of a coincidence.

He said, "Monny, I gotta go outside and make a quick call. Some interesting names popped up on this list, and I want to check them out." He took the list with him. On his cell he called Stennis's cell.

Harley answered.

"Harley, this is Denny Delaney. I hear you have George Bush and Arnold Palmer this month."

"Ha! You are a detective. Yeah, that's right. Are you in the same death pool we're in?"

"No, I'm in the Bubble Bath on Ninth, and I saw your names on the list. I didn't know you hung around here."

"I don't. My bar is The Flotsam near West 54th Street. I've known Paddy Shea for years, and he gets me in that pool. The pool at The Flotsam has a long waiting list."

"I was surprised to see you and Slattery's names on the list."

"Why? You going to nail us on a gambling charge?"

"No, of course not. It just seemed strange to see your names, that's all. I'm a-live-and-let live kind of guy."

"Me too. I also have a live-and-let-live philosophy."

"Of course, if you're in the death pool, you're hoping your famous pick will pass."

"Well, I guess that's life or death. Someone dies and someone profits. Anything else, Lieutenant?"

"No, that was all. Sorry to bother you."

"No problem. Stay healthy. Bye now. Keep the faith."

When Denny walked back into the bar, Wally was working the other end of the bar, and Bonny and Clyde were talking to Monny about Tiger Woods.

Denny contributed, "Tiger is lucky. He's way too young for the death pool."

28

Uniformed officers Ward and Mendoza were driving north on Third Avenue in their patrol car. At the corner of East 94th Street, they saw a black SUV parked illegally, lights on, motor idling. A man was crouched over in the street doing something. They had been briefed to be on the lookout for the Felix stenciler. The man spotted them, stood up and ran for the passenger door of the vehicle.

The two officers had a chance to see he'd been caught in the act of painting the message FELIX IS BACK on the street. Mendoza was on the police car's loudspeaker system.

"Police. Stop right now where you are. Now. Halt!"

The man jumped into the SUV, and it took off up the avenue at high speed. While Mendoza was on the PA system, Ward, at the wheel, raced the patrol car after the SUV. Mendoza radioed in their location and the details of the incident. He reported that the suspects were heading north on Third at high speed. All patrol cars in the area were alerted.

The SUV raced up the avenue, ran red lights, passed other vehicles maniacally, followed by the patrol car, sirens wailing and lights flashing. As the chase continued, Mendoza gave a running update on their location to the central communications center. When the SUV reached East 104th Street, it swerved around the corner, making a hard right. This turned out to be a big mistake. The street was obstructed by cars and trucks parked on both sides, with a UPS truck in the middle of the street completely blocking passage. There was no room to pass it. Ahead of the truck were stopped vehicles. A police patrol car with lights flashing was ahead, blocking any exit to Second Avenue heading south.

Mendoza and Ward drew out their automatics, rolled down their windows and waited to see if anyone would jump out of the trapped SUV. They played a waiting game.

Mendoza kept Central informed, and they could hear the sirens of more patrol cars coming in on both avenues. A cruiser pulled up in back of them, and the two officers in it got out, opened their trunk, and armed themselves with shot guns, then took up station behind Ward and Mendoza's vehicle.

Mendoza was on the horn again. "Police. Attention. You in the SUV. Come out of your vehicle now! Unarmed, with your hands above your head! No weapons! Now!"

Still no response. A waiting game began.

It was real piece of luck for Denny and Rich. They were about ten blocks from the incident in their vehicle when they heard the call come in. An SUV had stopped at a corner, and the "Felix Is Back" people had been spotted by a police patrol car. When the uniforms called it in, Denny and Rich had heard the call and were now racing up Third. Rich put the blue light on the roof and used his siren to rush to the location. Then they got word that the Felix SUV was trapped on a cross street, East 104th heading east, boxed in behind a truck, with police cars in front and in back.

NYPD cruisers were massing at both ends of the cross street. The blocked truck driver dashed out of his cab and scampered to safety in a store doorway as policemen, their weapons drawn, slowly edged from both avenues toward the SUV. Rich and Denny had pulled up on Third. With their weapons out, they joined the uniformed police closing in on the perp's vehicle. A SWAT team was on its way.

Mendoza continued to order the men out of the trapped SUV. It had heavily tinted windows so it was impossible to ascertain how many were inside.

Suddenly the passenger door opened, and a man armed with a handgun started running in a crouched position toward a storefront. Mendoza on the loudspeaker ordered the man to halt, but the fugitive kept going. Bullets rang out from all directions, and there was real danger of cops and civilians being caught in the crossfire. The man fell from the massive fuselage. When he was down, the shooting slowly petered out and stopped. No one approached the downed man, fearing they might become targets for whoever was left in the vehicle.

All the officers took cover again, and the waiting began as before. No action or movement from inside the SUV. The fallen man had left the passenger door open. There were no officers on the sides of the suspect vehicle to see inside.

The loudspeaker was roaring, "Exit your car and come out with your hands in the air."

Again, an unexpected move. The driver of the SUV put it in reverse and started backing at top speed toward the police cars behind it gathered at the corner of Third. Again a deafening and heavy volley of shots rang out, this time fired at the vehicle. The windows shattered and the reversing vehicle's tires were shot out. The backing SUV plowed into Mendoza and Ward's police car. The two vehicles went careening, hitting other cars like billiard balls on a pool table batting into one another.

When the cars had finished bashing and caroming into everything in their path, officers gingerly made their way toward the wrecks. In the suspect SUV the driver was found slumped over the steering wheel with his head swathed in blood. His face was a mess from gunshot wounds and the effects of the car crash. Officers assisted Mendoza and Ward, who were seriously injured but still conscious. Medics had rushed to them. One officer who had been behind their vehicle had suffered a shattered leg and nasty facial wounds. Two other officers were being treated for less serious injuries.

The scene was a madhouse: the two suspects were dead, police officers were being treated for injuries, crowds of onlookers had materialized from everywhere. Denny and Rich stayed at the scene until forensics had shown up to examine the damaged SUV.

A few days later Denny was meeting with Wexler in the FBI field office to get an update on the situation. Denny's friend, Agent Frank Millau sat in on the meeting.

Wexler said, "Denny, here's what we have so far. These two guys had ATM cards with the same account number and PIN number as Felix. It's a money market account with Chase without too much of a balance. No deposits have been made to the account since Felix's death, so whoever was supplying Felix's financial resources stopped contributing. The funds seemed to be coming from Lebanon although they could have originated anywhere in the world.

"These guys were probably the leftovers of Felix's cell. Apparently they thought they could stir up a little excitement by reigniting interest in Felix the Cat. We have an idea that they had no access to explosives, no contacts, no way of creating serious havoc. Only enough financial resources to live on for a limited time. Maybe they were awaiting orders from God knows who. Probably the dregs of the Felix gang. Dumb as shit, I would guess. It looks like they were the end of the line.

"We have no idea where they lived. The SUV had been leased over a year ago with phony documents, and monthly payments were coming in through money orders. The money came out of the money market account.

"CIA and all of the other intelligence agencies, as usual, are telling us squat. No help whatsoever. The fingerprints, DNA, photos, etcetera has been sent to Interpol, and so far like everything else, nada. We've checked every possible angle. We don't think the dead men were homegrown terrorists, but we have no way of knowing.

"We're sure that they had no connection with David, our vest bomber. It's another of those dead ends in this business. Sixteen intelligence agencies, and even Israel, come up with nothing. We're left with an SUV registered in a phony name to phony people, in a world of shadows."

Denny asked, "Do you think some of these intel agencies really know something and are holding back?"

"My own opinion? They aren't sharing the way they're supposed to. It's been called *stovepiping* where information in one agency goes up their stack, through their channels and just doesn't get shared.

"I long for the old days when the FBI was dealing with a guy like Dillinger, an independent contractor working for himself. It must have been great. No international contacts. No need to worry about some operator in Damascus supplying him with funds. Those were the old days of American homegrown capitalism and entrepreneurs."

"Yeah, Bruce, today everything is brutal. You should just be in my spot, just dealing with a serial killer who leaves no clues, no evidence, just deposits bodies and disappears into nowhere. Where is Jesse James when we really need him? For that matter, where's Wyatt Earp? Where's J. Edgar Hoover when life gets tough?"

"Denny, you and I were born in the wrong century."

"Do you mean the twentieth or the nineteenth?"

"Uh, probably in the nineteenth we would have been better off."

"But, Dude, if we lived in the nineteenth, who would be taking potshots at us outside the Palm Steak house on West Fiftieth Street?"

"Denny, you can never let that go, can you? You know what? Get the fuck out of my office before I send you to Cairo to be waterboarded."

"Bruce, as George Carlin would say with a smirk on his face, 'Have a nice day.'"

Denny reached over and shook Wexler's hand and gave a broadly smiling Frank a hug and headed for the door.

29

When Denny got closer to the crime scene this time, he could see the differences. This body had been dumped unceremoniously very close to the edge of the crumbling pier. The body bore no signs of being arranged, more like a rag doll that had been dropped from a height. Head off to a strange angle, one arm thrown out to the side, the other covered by the torso lying on its side. The legs were crossed and bent at the knees.

The body was shabbily dressed with filthy clothes, torn jeans, a grungy-looking stained baseball jacket. From his profile Denny could see that the man was in his early forties, his face bristling with several days of beard.

Rich and Terry had been at the scene for about a half hour. Terry said, "Looks like a bum to me. Definitely doesn't match any of the previous drops. The medical examiner, Dolores Ancino, said it was a homicide, but she didn't want to speculate on cause of death. He's got a bad bruise, a fresh one, on the back of his skull. No signs of strangulation. She said he's been dead at least eight hours. Couldn't determine whether the victim had been killed here or elsewhere."

Rich added, "Nothing seems to fit the profile of the others. Maybe perps are piling on, back to using waterfront drops again. And Denny, there's no condom in the mouth, and as you can see, the body wasn't laid out. The opposite, really just dumped. Lot of alcohol smell coming from on the guy. Also this guy doesn't fit our age group. For years bodies have been dumped at waterfront locations, and it may be that this one is part of the old tradition. An old habit that's come back to haunt us."

Denny said, "Any other thoughts, guys?"

Terry said, "If it's a copycat killing, the killer didn't even try to imitate any of the characteristics. Of course, it could be our guy trying to throw us off the track with an anomaly. But somehow I doubt it. This could very well be an isolated case. A random killing. Maybe the result of a drunken brawl. A case that has nothing to do with ours."

"Any ID? Anything on the body?" Denny asked.

Terry said, "Nothing in the pockets except junk Rich has in evidence bags. No jewelry. When they get him on the table, they may find tattoos, scars. He's been fingerprinted, so that may turn up something."

Denny said, "I think in the beginning we should do a full-court press, and then go on from there. Pretend at first that it's our guy who did it, and then we can always turn it over completely to Central Homicide. They'll be on the case anyhow. Or better yet, parallel investigations. Notify Madden and let him carry the ball from his end, and we'll follow up on our side. It could be that this guy knew something or saw something, and our guy had to get rid of him. Have Sex Crimes check photos just for the hell of it to see if they have a make on this guy."

Denny said to Rich, "Let's see what you found in the pockets."

Rich produced a plastic bag and read a list, "Fingernail clippers, a box of Tic Tacs, a bottle opener, a set of what looks like house keys, eighty-two cents in change, some penny coin wrappers, a bottle of superstrength Tylenol, three rubber bands, and two paper clips."

Denny rolled the corpse over so he could look at him full-face. Life had been tough for him. The face had some scars and wrinkles that indicated hard going. Denny knelt over him and could smell what he thought was bourbon. He looked at the man's hands and fingernails. Grimy hands, dirt under the nails. His hands would be bagged to discover if there had been any signs of a struggle, anything under the nails other than dirt.

Denny said, "For now let's call this the Odd Man Out case and go on the assumption it's ours temporarily. We'll work it as best we can, but let's see if Hal Madden can develop any leads."

The following Sunday was a beautiful clear day. Denny

and Monny were sitting in their breakfast nook. She was working on her laptop, and he was doing the *Times* Sunday magazine crossword puzzle.

He looked up and said, "Monny, how would you like to go on the Circle Line tour around Manhattan today?"

"I'd love it. Great idea. Wait a minute, do you have a hidden agenda here? I always suspect you of some devious motive."

"Well, in a way, I do. One of our techies made me up a map of Manhattan with the sites marked where our serial killer placed his victims. I wanted to take along some binoculars and see if I can scope out some pattern or who knows what from the water perspective."

"That doesn't sound like it will interfere with my enjoying the trip. We haven't been on that tour in years. Yeah, let's go, Sherlock."

Later they walked west on their street to Twelfth Avenue, turned south and headed toward the Circle Line Pier Number 83 at 42nd Street.

They sat on the top level of the excursion boat for the three-hour circumnavigation of Manhattan Island. The narrator named Oscar was a comedian and a wise guy, but he packed his talk with a great deal of information. Oscar told everyone over the PA system that they would see twenty bridges and traverse three rivers: the Hudson, the East, and the Harlem which he said was known as both a river and as a ship canal. On the trip Denny was busy with his large map and his binoculars. Monny just enjoyed the trip and the pleasant breezes blowing off the waterways.

As they headed south down the Hudson River, Oscar pointed out the important sites and the new buildings. Passing the World Trade Center site, he gave a very respectful and thorough account of the Nine-Eleven tragedy.

Entering the expanse of Upper New York Bay, the ship eased closer to the Statue of Liberty so people could take good photos. After the Staten Island ferry terminal, they headed up the East River.

At the Manhattan Bridge Oscar pointed out the DUMBO section, and explained that the acronym meant "Down under the Manhattan Brooklyn Overpass." They continued on up the East River with Oscar's narration in the background. When they got to the Harlem River, Denny saw one of the drop sites quite close to the boat.

At Spuyten Duyvil, they turned and headed south down the Hudson toward their taking-off point. Opposite streets in the West Sixties, Oscar began the story of the US Airways jet that had made an emergency landing in the river on January 15th of 2009. It was the event that had kept Denny and Monny glued to their television sets that historic day. He described the plane coming down between West 48th Street and Weehawken, New Jersey. The Circle Line boats, ferry boats, and police and fire boats, he proudly explained, had rushed to the rescue and saved all of the passengers that day. His account added drama to the trip, and people on the first deck watched a televised recounting of the famous event.

When they were getting ready to disembark, Monny turned to Denny and said, "Did you guys ever consider the possibility that your perp was dropping off these bodies by using a boat and coming and going by water just as we did?"

Denny replied, "Oh, my God, you may have hit on something I never thought about. Out of the mouths of babes . . ."

30

Denny, his father, mother and Monny were at the bar in The Old Florida Seafood House on Northeast Twenty-sixth Street in Wilton Manors, not far from his parents' home in the Coral Ridge section of Fort Lauderdale. Denny and his father had been swapping baseball talk with Don, the white-haired bartender from Philadelphia. Don walked to the other end of the bar to serve a party of four that had just come in from outside.

His father leaned over so Monny and Carole couldn't hear. "I'm expecting a call from a retired buddy of mine from the Department. His son's serving now. He may have some information for me to pass on to you. It might be about your serial-killer case. I'll let you know by tomorrow."

The next night Denny, Monny, and Denny's parents were at the bar in Chuck's Steakhouse on Commercial Boulevard near Federal Highway. Carole and Eamon loved to eat out. Having lived on Restaurant Row for years, Carole's cooking skills were limited. At least that's what she claimed as her defense for wanting to eat out. Denny's dad was very tired from his recent chemo regimen that had been wearing him down.

For his dad, Denny fetched a plate of salad from the salad bar in the restaurant section in the big room of the restaurant. After all these years, he knew what his father liked. While his father munched on the salad, Denny had a crock of chicken gumbo soup. The two women were sipping their merlots and gossiping about Broadway stuff. Monny and Carole had both seen the long-running musical *Wicked* and couldn't understand the show's attraction or staying power.

Eamon smiled at Denny, and Denny knew his father wanted to say something out of the wives' earshot. Eamon said, "Den, don't let your loyalty to the Department cloud your judgment."

"What brings that on, Dad?"

"I've been following the river homicides. Let your instincts lead wherever they take you, you hear me? Even if it involves cops."

"Oh, I will, don't worry about that."

"Twisted cops, Den, are a fact of life, unfortunately. Sometimes they cover things up, and sometimes they're directly involved. They see so much shit, they sometimes get warped, go off the track. They get to be as bad as the people they're hunting. Why should a badge make them any different from anyone else? Same impulses, same pressures. The badge should keep them on the straight and narrow, but it can give empowerment, a sense of entitlement. Sometimes they take shortcuts. They can be sickos like anyone else. Believe me, in all my years on the force, I saw plenty. Lots of bad apples. Of course a lot of good, honest guys, but . . ."

Denny turned to his father, "Have you heard something from one of your old buddies on the force about the river homicides?"

"Kinda, indirectly. The father of a kid who's on the force now said his kid told him that there may be an insider involved."

"Who? Give me details."

"Hey, Den, if I knew anything pertinent, anything specific, I'd tell you. This may only be someone spouting off. Just rumors. The gossip filtered down to me. I can't tell you any more, can't give you any names. I don't want my friend's kid getting hurt.

"Den, certain things don't ring true. I'm worried about those lousy e-mails that Monny got. But I'm way away from the action now. Long gone, but I feel things. Bad vibes. Hey, good salad. I like these olives, the cherry tomatoes, and the Russian dressing. That flat bread is a good choice too, kiddo. You sure can make my kind of salad.

"But, Den, wherever the trail in this thing leads, follow up on it, even if people in the Department are involved. Somebody's got to pay for those poor kids' deaths. They were only kids."

"Don't worry, if cops are in on this, they'll pay like anyone else."

"Son, don't try to wipe him out. See if you can bring him to trial. Use the system—that's what it's for. You have a tendency—hey, I'm sorry to have to say this, but you have an inclination to act as prosecutor, judge, jury, and executioner. Don't lose your perspective in this case."

"Jeez, Dad, you make me sound like a monster, a vindictive SOB. Hey, Dad, I'm more cautious than you think. I'm not over-the-top on this stuff."

"I know, Den, just stay as objective as you can."

"Dad, I promise."

"Sonny boy, you *are* zealous. I think you get impatient with the justice system and like to grease the skids, but, you know what, you do whatever you have to do to make things right. You know what you're doing, and whatever happens, happens, right?"

Then the two couples all joined in a conversation because of Carole's prodding, and they had a good time for the rest of the evening.

That night at his parents' home after they had gotten back from the restaurant, Denny got a call on his cell from Tim.

"Denny, they're on to me. They're after me."

"Who? Why do you say *they*?"

"Because I get the feeling there's more than one killer."

"How do you know?"

"Cars with windows heavily tinted, following, turning up on the streets tracking me."

"What kind of cars?"

"Different ones. More than one kind."

"What makes, what years?"

"How the fuck do I know? I can't tell one car from the other. Listen, Denny, I'm in P'Town. I'll be up here for a week. I know a guy who can hide me out, keep me safe temporarily. Can you come up and see me?"

"P'Town on the Cape?"

"Yeah, of course on the Cape. Where else?"

"Where are you staying?"

"It's a small town. You'll find me, or I'll find you. I'll be in and out of the gay bars—the A House, the Crown and Anchor, the Gifford House. I'll be in George's Pizza across from Town Hall from time to time. Walk along Commercial Street. I'll spot you. Believe me, I'll find you."

"Can you be more specific as to an address?"

"No, we'll find each other. Can you get me into some kind of protective custody?"

"Yes. Definitely."

"See you, Denny. If you don't come and see me, I'll be a dead man."

"I'll be up there tomorrow."

Denny told Monny about the call. She was doubtful. "Do you think you really have to go there? Is it really necessary? I'll miss you."

"Monny, I'm driving on empty with this case. I need any glimmer of information I can get. Something to ignite the case, or otherwise we're going to be facing a hopeless mess."

31

Denny took an early-morning Jet Blue flight from Fort Lauderdale to Boston. Across from the Jet Blue gate at Logan was the gate to Cape Air which flew up to Provincetown. Later he climbed aboard the nine-passenger twin-engine Cessna for the twenty-minute flight up to P'Town. The pilot welcomed Denny to sit next to him in the copilot's seat. From there he had a stunning view at three thousand feet above the harbor and the beginning of the Cape. For about ten minutes the plane passed mile after mile of coastal cottages and houses. Then the plane was over open water heading through thick fog to the hook of the Cape where P'Town nestled in its sheltered harbor.

The high Pilgrim Monument tower came into sight, then as they got closer, stretches of golden sand along the shoreline with beach buggies, fishing poles protruding from the sand, and off to the side the desolate moors. A lighthouse, then the small runway in the middle of nowhere. The plane landed at a slow speed, bumped once lightly, taxied down one runway, made a right turn and then rolled down another strip to the terminal.

Denny climbed down the shaky metal steps built into the door and headed for the small terminal where he was greeted by a welcoming golden retriever who loved to schmooze with people. Denny waited for his bag to be unloaded from a bow cavity.

One woman was working at the tiny check-in counter. Denny asked her to call for a taxi. Denny waited outside. A small parking lot in front of the terminal was loaded with the cars of people who had flown out. A Range Rover pulled up. On the side was written Tallulah's Cab Co. The driver wasn't very informative; he was from the Czech Republic, driving cabs for his second summer, but thankfully he knew Denny's destination.

The cab brought him to his guesthouse, The Captain's Nookie, on Commercial Street across from the Boatslip Hotel, where gay tea dances were held from four to seven on the expansive deck hanging over the harbor beach and the tranquil bay. The house was an old Victorian beauty with a spacious front porch and bay windows. It was rose-colored with gray trim.

Barney, the owner of the guesthouse, a paunchy six-foot bearded man in his forties, greeted him.

He said, "Welcome to The Captain's Nookie. A stupid name, but shit, we inherited the name when we bought the place, and our clients have been coming here for years, so if it ain't broken, don't even try to fix it. We kept the name, kept most of the customers. Breakfast in the dining room is from eight to eleven. We're making fresh blueberry muffins tomorrow morning. Enjoy yourself. If you need anything just call me, my lover Harris or Bobbie, the houseboy. Welcome aboard the Captain's Nookie, matey."

Barney led him up the steep staircase to his room on the second floor. His dog, a pug, followed them puffing laboriously as it maneuvered up the stairs and waited in the hall. The owner showed him the essentials including a communal desktop computer in the alcove, gave him a quick tour of the room and then took off, his dog dutifully following him back down the stairs.

A high, four-poster king-sized bed dominated the small over-decorated room. The nineteenth century house had been renovated by the addition of private bathrooms. The room's closet had been converted to a bath, and a large wardrobe became a substitute for a closet.

A flat-screen TV had been mounted on the wall opposite the bed that was piled high with pillows and bolsters. Every spare inch of the room was covered with kitschy stuff and antiques. Denny thought the only thing the room lacked was space for the lodger to move around. One nightstand with an oak front that resembled an old two-door ice box was a small refrigerator with bottled water and complimentary health drinks. Denny unpacked and relaxed for a while before heading out on the street.

When he walked outside into the hall, he saw on a table next to the usual gay rag bar magazines, an overflowing bowl of condoms wrapped in blue plastic. They were identical to the ones found on the bodies. That wasn't unusual because millions had been distributed. He grabbed a handful and stuffed them into his jeans pocket, hoping for analysis. Maybe the lab people could find similarities. There were scores of gay guesthouses in Provincetown, and all of them probably gave away the identical product. And the gay bars, restaurants and shops as well.

Denny walked down the steep stairway and hung a right for a walk up Commercial Street heading toward the West End, the Provincetown Inn and the moors. He had been in P'Town several times before but had not been back for a few years. He knew the general layout of the town. The old Victorian houses, beautifully kept and well cared for by house-proud owners had manicured lawns and lush gardens which in spring and summer would have flowers everywhere: geraniums, petunias, and roses. The flowers flourished in the salt air with the pervasive mists that blanketed the town at night. Denny passed guesthouses, many with nautical names, antique shops, real estate offices, coffee places, touristy shops, then a long series of private homes. The sidewalk was uneven and treacherous for the unwary. Some sections were brick, some asphalt, and some cement.

The town was full of rainbow flags, dog walkers, bicyclists, young guys showing off their pecs, cats disdainfully with regal grace strolling across the streets. The native Portuguese population was slowly being driven out by the high real estate prices and gentrification.

As Denny headed toward the Provincetown Inn at the west end of Commercial Street, he passed the Coast Guard Station with its pier pushing far out into the harbor. He walked past Sal's Italian Restaurant on the waterside and later the Red Inn, also a waterfront place.

Some of the people passing said hello, something that unnerved a native New Yorker like Denny. Perhaps somewhere along the street as he walked, he would see or be seen by Tim.

Opposite the sprawling Provincetown Inn was a small traffic circle. In the center was a park containing a group of embedded memorial stones placed in memory of the dead who had either lived in P'Town or had had some association with it.

A long breakwater, more than one-half mile long, made of giant stones, granite-like, reached out and formed a bridge to the ocean beach. Denny had no time to go out on the wall, so he turned and headed back along Commercial Street toward the center of town, glancing at the private homes and guesthouses as he passed, hoping that Tim might have sussed him out. That first day and night he caught no sight of Tim.

Days passed with no sign of him. While he was staying in P'Town, Denny haunted the Mayflower Café on Commercial Street, a fixture in town since 1929, a place favored by locals because of its reasonably priced and vast variety of good food. Denny could always find something for lunch or dinner on the extensive menu that featured all kinds of food, but particularly fresh local fish, or what had been local fish before the banks off the coast got fished out.

There was plenty of comfort food, regional specialties, Portuguese and Italian dishes. Denny had a hard time deciding among chicken croquettes, hot turkey sandwiches, codfish cakes, meatball subs, fried clams, lobster roll, and so many more dishes. Denny would usually order Indian pudding for dessert because it was so alien to New York menus.

On the menu it said, "Tipping is Customary. Big Tips are greatly appreciated."

Denny liked to order the fried-fish dishes now that Monny wasn't looking. She kept an eye on his cholesterol and fat intake. He could order fried scallops, fried clams with the bellies, scrod or the combo fried plate. The white clam chowder and Portuguese kale soup with linguica and red kidney beans were great treats.

He'd get a small booth to himself on the bar side. They had a full liquor bar, but Denny limited himself to one glass of rosé. No one bothered him. Some of the help were from eastern Europe. His usual waiter was from Bulgaria, one of the workers who came into town for the summer season. They had a big enough menu to keep Denny busy for weeks, but time was running short. In phone calls home, he could tell Monny was getting antsy, irritated by his absence.

She cracked, "It must be tough investigating in a resort town. Don't bring any bedbugs back. We've got enough of the homegrown variety right now in New York. They're the leading topic on my blog."

At Ciro and Sal's down an alley in the East End he had one big Italian dinner of veal parmigiana and spaghetti on a platter. He ate in Napi's and the Lobster Pot because after all Provincetown was full of great restaurants, but most of the time he haunted the Mayflower.

One night early, Denny was sitting in a dark alcove in the A House, probably one of the world's most famous gay bars. The place hadn't changed much in many decades. It was still dark and creepy looking to Denny, with the jukebox playing old Billie Holiday records, the fireplace with a tree-trunk stump next to it, the crooked bar stools cemented into the floor, the two small windows letting a little light in from Kiley Court.

While Denny was sitting there, thinking he'd never see him in P'Town, Tim hurried in, just putting away a cell phone. He looked around furtively, saw Denny and sat down at one of the wrought-iron ice cream parlor chairs opposite him. Looking the worse for wear, he began right away, "Denny, I'm in deep shit. They have my cell number. They're following me. Don't ask me who. I don't know. I want to live, I want to survive. These creeps are out to get me."

"Why do you say *they*, more than one?"

"Just a creepy feeling I got, that's all. They, he, she, whoever, they're going to get me, and you can't seem to do shit to stop them. I just feel it. My days are numbered."

"Calm down. What are you talking about?"

"I'm on their list. They're closing in on me."

Denny said, "Tell me what you've heard or seen."

"I've heard scuttlebutt. A couple of my street buddies in the city said they heard I'm next."

"Why you?"

"'Cause the word is out I been talking to the cops, to you in particular."

"How would *they* know?"

"Hey, you're asking me? Maybe you been leaking to your press buddies."

"Uh-uh. Never happen. If I did that, everyone loses. This couple of guys that gave you information? Are your buddies in touch with the killers?"

"No, just things they heard on the street."

"Yeah, rumors, gossip, speculation. People like to act like they're in the know."

"I've got to stay on the run. I got some older buddies, johns, who can protect me for a while up here."

Denny shoved a wad of papers across to Tim.

"Tim, here's a photocopy of the address book we found on Manuel Guiterrez's body. Take it, look at it when you have a chance. Study it and see if anything clicks. If it does, let me know."

"Okay. Gotta go. Denny, they're probably following you. You're probably on their list too. We're both dead men. Look, I've got to get back to the city. I've got a ride lined up. The less I'm seen with you, the better it is for both of us."

"Wait. Why don't you stay up here. You're much safer here than in New York."

"If they don't kill me, cabin fever will get me. I wanna be back where the action is, the clubs, the hectic life style. Look, Denny, you're the greatest. I'm relying on you. I'll stay in close touch, don't worry."

Denny was embarrassed when Tim got up and gave him a quick but intimate hug.

Tim was out the door so fast that Denny had no time to stop him for a few more words. He practically ran out into the alley.

Denny left P'Town on an early flight the next morning.

32

Denny and Monny were at Sardi's in the upstairs bar talking to Joe, the bartender, about recent horse races. Jake Sigman walked in accompanied by a knock-dead blonde chorine. Jake saw Denny, and Denny saw him, but both avoided direct eye contact.

Jake had been cleared of any involvement in the murders, but Denny had never sought a reconciliation or given Jake the courtesy of telling him he'd been cleared. Denny knew that Jake's lawyer had notified his client, so he felt he owed him nothing. And Jake had been damn insulting that day. His personal insults still stung.

Jake was sitting at the other end of the bar. Denny had previously told Monny that he and Jake had a falling-out but hadn't explained any more. Some friends came over and chatted with Denny and his wife. Time passed.

Later Jake and his date, heading for a table, passed by Denny. Jake stopped and said hello to Monny and gave her a peck on the cheek. He offered his hand to Denny saying, "Den, we're both pros. We both have codes we have to follow no matter what. Don't think I don't understand the stress and strain you've been under with these murder cases. Just remember that I said things in the heat of the moment that I deeply regret. That's me. Your old man and I have short fuses. Give me a break. I still love you and your dad and always will. We go back a long way together, all of us. You're known as an avenging angel when you're on a case. Here, give me a big hug."

Denny, his eyes tearing up, stood and gave Jake a heartfelt hug. Then Jake hugged Monny. He winked at Monny and said, "Hon, you have a handful with this stud, but, you know what, he's worth it."

Jake and his date then proceeded to their table. Jake

seemed to be shuffling along, showing his age.

Monny said, "He's always been a great friend. He seems to have aged in the last year."

"Yeah, haven't we all."

Monny said, "I'm glad you two are back on speaking terms. Your dad and Jake go back a long way."

"Yeah, hon, I'm glad that Jake and I can talk again."

The next day Denny was sitting in his office going over some reports, when his landline rang. It was Hal Madden.

"Denny, I've got some interesting stuff and some good leads. Victim Number Seven, our Odd Man Out Case. We showed the guy's photos to some of our midtown people. We've got a make on this guy. They recognized him, and I tracked down one of his drinking buddies who led me to a bunch of others. The victim was Tony Angelli. A rummy, a barfly, and a guy who did odd jobs, not always legit ones. Hung around in a lot of midtown saloons. Played pool for drinks and small change. Wasn't gay, didn't hustle. Sure, he hustled up booze and smokes and crap jobs, but didn't hustle his buns.

"When we tracked down his buddies, we came up with a long list of drinking establishments, none classy or elegant, mostly dives, you understand. Want me to read the list?"

"Yeah, Hal, it can't hurt. I may have even frequented a few myself."

"Okay. Timmy's Topside, The Clover Wheel, Jocko's, The Isle of Mandy . . ."

Denny's cell phone rang. He said, "Hold it a minute, Hal, I've got to take this."

It was a woman from Media Relations who had a quick question. Denny answered it and resumed his talk with Hal.

"Sorry, Hal. Go ahead."

"The Wee Hours, Sandy's Harbor View, the Dew Drop Inn, The Flotsam, The Crazy Course, O'Rooney's, Sam and Natalies, and the Cooing Dove."

"Sounds like every dump in midtown."

"Now, here's the interesting part, Denny, maybe even what

might be the clincher. The lab boys have been working on fibers found on the victims' clothing. They've found a match between what they believe to be carpet fibers from a vehicle. They have matched up fibers from Victim Three and our Odd Man Out. A definite match. That proves that with all of the evidence to the contrary, our boy Tony was killed by the same guy that did Number Three and the other hustlers."

"In other words, Hal, our Odd Man Out was thrown into the mix to sidetrack us. He wasn't arranged or staged, there was no condom in the mouth, and no strangulation, but the lab guys have been able to tie these killings in together. Why would our hustler killer do this? Kill the Odd Man Out?"

"Denny, it could be a perverted sense of humor. Throwing us off stride. Oh, and by the way. The lab says that they can't find any other fiber matches, but they are going to try and track which car manufacturers might have used this type of carpeting."

"Hal, please e-mail me your whole report, everything you've just told me so I can go through it with Terry and Rich."

"I'll send the stuff right away."

"And Hal, you and your guys and the lab people did great work. Thank you very much. I'll be sure that The Pigmy gives you full credit."

"Thanks, Denny. It's nice to feel needed again."

33

Denny decided to consult with one of his former college profs at Fordham. He had taken a course on criminal psychology with Dr. Gregory Estermass. They met outside on a bench on the Fordham campus. It was always like old home week for Denny visiting the school, because he had spent four years there. Estermass was a devout and dogmatic Roman Catholic. Estermass allotted Denny as much time as he needed to present the info.

He had become somewhat of an expert on serial killers. Police departments and the FBI consulted him regularly.

He was extremely thin, either anorexic or else his metabolism was hyperactive. He had close-set, deeply embedded eyes, but a nose larger than it should have been.

He was a chain-smoker, which might have been responsible for his emaciated state.

Denny had brought a thick file of documents. He showed Estermass pictures of the bodies taken in situ. He had a sample wrapped condom with him, and showed pictures of the condoms found on the victims. He described the way each body had been carefully arranged, laid out.

Denny said, "Medical opinion seems to agree that they were all strangled from behind. I'm, of course, going to leave this stuff with you so you can study it at your leisure."

The doctor read over various reports, studied other photos and with a cigarette hanging from his mouth said, "I think we're dealing with a sociopath here rather than a psychopath. He hasn't gone off the deep end yet. He's still on the reservation. He has a job somewhere. He's functioning, working, and doing this on the side.

"I've looked at dates, times, etcetera, and a pattern doesn't jump out at me yet. He picks the waterfront drops because they are spread out all over the city and are convenient to get to in a vehicle; I don't see any deep symbolic significance to location. The fact they are the waterside, I think, does not mean anything. Remember, Denny, I'm not psychic, and I use a lot of guesswork. This isn't a science; it's strictly amateurish bullshit.

"But I do believe that your guy or gal is still with it. Hasn't snapped quite yet, and I would judge isn't the type to snap unless he were under a great deal of pressure.

"The bodies, I think, are laid out in a respectful manner because the victims in the mind of the killer are only partly responsible for what they did."

Denny asked, "What did they do?"

"Let me think about it. They were naughty but still nice. Get it?"

"No."

"I think 'naughty but nice' might be key to this guy's thinking. They're guilty, these victims, but with extenuating circumstances. They're only kids after all, but what they did was bad, so they have to be punished. They will be denied supper, but they'll get a full breakfast. Get it? Being punished, but with a chance of redemption. It could be that the killer is a religious nut wanting to wake his victims like a funeral director. Hey, we're dealing with a nutso here. Functioning, but still a looney tune. Before I forget, let me add that a lot of these serial-killer creatures were involved in animal abuse when they were younger."

Another cigarette appeared.

"Now, the safeties, the rubbers, the scumbags. If one of these kids had worn a rubber, then maybe something like disease might have been prevented. The rubber, I think, is to tell the other kids still out there, 'Next time, wear a rubber before it's too late.' I think the rubbers are reminders that the kids haven't played it safe. The condoms tie the killings together.

"In a way, they are totemic, more of a signature, but I think they are just reminders of what can go wrong if you're not practicing safe sex. I think that these kids are being knocked off because hustlers in general don't use condoms. I don't think particular kids are being targeted, but I have a feeling that the killer knows who he's going after.

"Also, your man is a pro. He doesn't leave forensic evidence. Judging from a brief look at these reports, there's no sexual interference, no mutilation, which makes me more inclined to say he's a sociopath. No mutilation, but decoration which in serial killer lingo refers to decorating the corpse, in this case with a condom in the mouth and arranging the bodies in a formal or ritualistic manner. Bear in mind the way I use sociopath and psychopath, they're both nutters. Just degrees of nuttiness and taking into account the ability to function without going off the deep end.

"One danger from a police standpoint is that your guy could stop any time and just quit. It could all come to an end. He could get bored or scared off. Move to another part of the country, kill himself, or just stop and retire from this stuff. Now let me look at those e-mails. I want to read them carefully."

Denny handed Estermass copies of the two e-mails sent to Monny. He read them carefully. Another cigarette. *How many packs did he carry around with him?* Denny wondered.

"Let's do some thinking here. How do you know, how do I know we're dealing with a serial killer as we sit here? Because of similarities: the location of the victims by waterways, the way they are uniformly laid out, the condoms, the cause of death, the ages and so-called occupations of the victims. All of these items let us know we're dealing with a serial killer, a person who repeats certain elements of his murders.

"But for what purpose are the e-mails? To demean you, to stick it to you, to ire Monica? Yes. But to scare you off? No. Are they a cry for help? No. Are they intended to start a dialogue between you and the killer? No. Are they a method for the killer and you to bond, to be as one to wrap you in victimhood so you can share the guilt? No, I don't see it that way.

"My supposition would be they serve no purpose for the killer, and only put him at greater risk for no reason. I think they are the product of another party entirely. I believe you are dealing with two entities. One is the killer. The other is someone sending the e-mails."

Denny asked, "Two separate people? A killer and the e-mail writer?"

"My guess is yes. Someone guilty of a criminal act in sending such nasty stuff to Monica, but not guilty of the murders. A wise guy. A know-it-all. A wannabe guy, not a killer but someone who really hates your guts. Is envious of you. Feels you're a threat. Not as smart as he thinks he is.

"I think if your serial killer gets hold of this e-mail writer, he'll kill him, throttle him, and he'll be the next corpse you find. Probably with a printer cartridge stuffed in his mouth instead of a condom. Only my opinion, understand. Nothing definite. I don't see your serial killer as an epistolarian.

"In the e-mails the writer brings up your alcoholism, demeans you, attacks your masculinity on the one hand and reminds Monny of it in relation to Terry Kerrigan. He knows details of the investigation, the whereabouts of your father, and knows a lot about the lives of you and Monny.

"Calling the killer the Kondom Killer doesn't show great originality or the talent for coming up with a memorable name, a tag. Did you notice he never says that he is the Kondom Killer, never takes credit for being the killer? That would really cook his goose if he got caught as the writer.

"Denny, leave all this stuff with me and give me time to percolate with this material, and I'll get back to you."

The psychologist stalked away with a new cigarette dangling from his mouth. He had sent something seething in Denny's mind.

34

Denny thought Monny's sister was a pain in the butt. *The most dependent broad I've ever seen. She's got Monny on a short leash, and every once in a while she yanks it. Monny is a sucker for her sister's tearful stories.*

Monny's sister and her husband were always having marital troubles, and the sister leaned on Monny when she was despondent. Her husband had taken off for points unknown again, and Monny had gone out to Mineola on Long Island to stay with her sister for a few nights, so Denny was on his own.

At ten o'clock he was in the apartment watching a black-and-white *Thin Man* movie starring Myrna Loy and William Powell, a favorite flick of his dad's. It was raining outside, coming down very hard, the rain pelting the windows. A strong wind was blowing through the 46th Street canyon from the Hudson River. The building was an ancient brownstone so old that the windows shook and rattled in the wind and rain.

The doorbell rang.

Denny grabbed his Walther pistol and went down to the front door. He peered through the peephole. In the dim light he could see Tim. He opened the door.

"What the hell are you doing here?"

"Delaney, please let me in."

Denny opened the door and ushered him in. Tim was wearing a light jacket and was soaked. Denny looked up and down the street, but it was impossible to see if there was anyone watching the house. His usual security detail was probably out there, but Tim could have been followed.

While Tim was going up the stairs, Denny called his security-alert number which put him in contact with the officers watching his house. They had seen Tim come up to the door and had seen Denny letting him in, but they hadn't seen any strange cars keeping track of Denny's visitor.

He led Tim to his apartment door.

Tim asked, "Anyone else home? The missus?"

"No, I'm alone right now. You're soaked. Where you been?"

"On the run."

"From who?"

"I don't know. I just know they're after me. I made sure I wasn't followed here though. I'm at the end of my rope. I know they're going to get me."

"Why do you keep saying *they*?"

"Because this time I saw two guys watching me from a car when I got back from P'Town."

Denny fetched a big white terry cloth cotton bathrobe that had Celebrity Cruise Lines stitched across the back, and handed it to Tim.

"You should take off those wet clothes. You're soaked to the skin. Why don't you go in the bathroom, get out of those clothes, take a hot shower and put this on."

Tim went into the bathroom, and soon Denny heard water running. He was in there a long time. Denny felt uneasy. He was glad that Monny wasn't home. Tim was an unknown quantity. He didn't like the idea of Tim, a hustler, in his house—especially when he was taking a shower and about to come out of the bathroom wearing just a bathrobe. Tim's hug in Provincetown had spooked him.

Denny thought, *I've got to get rid of him, but I can't put him out on those rainy streets and in danger. Go outside and face God knows what. Maybe I should call Rich and have Tim taken to the local precinct for safekeeping. Having Rich know he's in the house doesn't appeal to me though. Maybe later call a cab and take him myself somewhere for safekeeping. I could even get the FBI to keep him safe in the field office.*

If he let him go out on his own, he might be putting him at risk. Calling Rich or Terry was problematic because they had never met Tim, and Denny might be opening himself up to something that he'd have difficulty explaining.

When Tim finally came out of the steam-filled bathroom, the bathrobe was partially open and Denny saw a flash of nude flesh and pubic hair before Tim pulled it closed and tied the cotton belt. He looked very young and vulnerable. He had shaved. His blond hair, still wet, was neatly combed. He looked like a college kid on spring break in Fort Lauderdale. *That was a weird thing to think about. Shit, "Where the Boys Are" is playing in my brain.*

"Well, Mr. Delaney, you've got a nice place here. Kind of old-fashioned and sixtyish but still nice. I'll bet it's rent-controlled."

Rent control was a subject that almost every New Yorker thought about or asked about. It was like having a license to steal or print your own money to many New Yorkers.

"Yeah, still rent-controlled."

"From?"

"My parents."

"That figures. Oh, great, a cop with big bucks in a rent-controlled apartment. What a racket."

"I don't know where you get the big bucks part. I'm still a civil servant on a city stipend."

"Yeah, I can imagine what a lieutenant pulls down. And all that overtime. What about all that dough you made from selling your story to the movies, the story about Felix the Cat?"

"That went mainly to my friend the author, as it should have. And then to his widow after he was murdered by Felix."

"You don't mind being called Denny, do you?"

"No, be my guest. I told you that in the Tiffany Diner, remember?"

"Okay. Denny. You're a hunk, you know that. You'd make some guy a nice poppy."

Denny was very embarrassed by Tim's comments.

"Tim, let's just stick to business here, okay?"

"Yeah, sure, I'm in danger of ending up a river corpse, and you feel threatened by a hustler in your house, and you're giving me straight static. Trying to protect your straight genes. While I'm trying to save my life, you're playing Mr. Heterosexual."

"Tell me what's been going on since P'Town."

"I should have stayed there. I have a lot of friends up there who could have kept me safe for as long as I wanted. I was stupid coming back to the city. Now I'm being followed again by, I think, the killers."

"More than one, you're sure?"

"Yeah, two of them. And don't ask me what they look like, because they have tinted windows."

"A car, SUV, or van?"

"It's not always the same."

"How do you know that these guys are the killers?"

"What the fuck. Do you think I'm an idiot? Oh, Denny, where's Mrs. Delaney, your better half?"

"She's visiting her sister for the night."

"Oh, great, we can bond, just us guys. Hey, Denny, I'm starving, do you mind if I look in your kitchen and refrigerator to see if I can rustle up some food. Are you hungry?"

"Don't worry about me. Be my guest. Whatever you can find to eat, you're welcome to. Just do your own thing."

Tim came back in a few minutes.

"Den, do you like omelets? I found eggs, cheese, mushrooms, peppers, ham, and bread for toast. How 'bout I make us some omelets?"

"Okay, if you want."

"You just sit down and watch TV or something, and I'll cook us a snack."

After Tim had finished preparing the food, they sat opposite each other in the booth of the breakfast nook off the kitchen. Tim had turned off the overhead kitchen light, and subdued light came from two sconces in the nook.

It was a very artful presentation. He had used Monny's white china oblong dishes. The omelet was neatly arranged on one side with a sprig of parsley. He had cut a tomato in half and broiled it with some bread crumbs and cheese bits.

Thin cucumber slices lined one side of the plate. He had placed half slices of wheat toast on each plate.

Denny thought that Tim had either been a waiter in a good restaurant or perhaps worked in an upscale kitchen as a sous-chef.

Tim said, "You have a great kitchen. It's been remodeled fairly recently, all high-end appliances, and your wife has all the tools and equipment. Does your wife like to cook?"

"Yes, she does enjoy cooking, but because we know so many restaurateurs we eat out a lot."

"What's her name, your wife?"

"Monica, but everyone calls her Monny."

"Would you like some coffee? A glass of wine?"

"No, thank you. I'm supposed to take it easy on my drinking, and coffee at night keeps me awake."

"In your kitchen I saw a wine rack with a nice selection of wines. Would you mind if I open a red and have a glass?"

"No, no, please be my guest. Pick out any bottle that meets your fancy."

Tim got up, selected a bottle and took a goblet down from an overhead rack. "Dennis, I picked out a merlot. Where's the wine opener?"

"The top left-hand drawer next to the stove."

Denny noticed how professionally Tim uncorked the bottle, efficiently and effortlessly.

"Were you a waiter?"

"Yeah, for a while. Also I got a lot of experience with a certain elderly john who has since passed away, unfortunately. A terrific human being. Oh, and by the way, in case you've been trying to get some background on me, my full name is Tim O'Neill."

"Thank you, Tim O'Neill, for trusting me."

Tim placed the bottle on the table, poured himself a glassful and then sat down again and attacked his meal. Denny found the omelet to be delicious with ham, cheese, and mushrooms.

Tim said, "Monny certainly stocks a lot of food even though she doesn't cook at home that often."

"Oh, she always has plenty of fresh stuff for when she gets in the mood."

"Are you sure you wouldn't like a little wine?"

"Uh, maybe a little."

Tim jumped up and got him a glass. He poured a decent quantity in the glass and placed it in front of Denny who swirled the wine around and took a taste. It was a decent merlot. Tim was still wearing the bathrobe, which made Denny uneasy.

Denny said, "How 'bout I rustle you up a pair of Levis and a shirt while your stuff is drying?"

"No, I'm fine. I turned on the ceiling heater in the bathroom, so my stuff should dry out fairly fast."

Tim had very quickly finished everything on his plate.

"You must have been hungry."

"Very. I've had little time to think about eating. I noticed some Häagen-Dazs mango ice cream in the freezer. Would you like some?"

"No, but you go ahead."

"Monny won't mind someone raiding her kitchen?"

"Of course not. It could have been me doing the raiding, you know."

Tim brought back a large dish of ice cream which he quickly demolished.

Denny said, "If you're still hungry, have anything you want."

"No, I'm fine now. I didn't have anything to eat all day. I've been too hyper."

Denny had finished his food. "Tim, you're a great cook. This was great."

"As good as Monny's?"

"Almost."

Denny rose and started to carry the plates and utensils to the sink. Tim took them from him.

Tim said, "No, Big Guy, you just go in the living room and sit down. I'll have all this cleaned up in a jiff. Go ahead. Relax. I'll take care of this stuff. Would you like to watch a DVD? I notice you have a big collection."

"Boy, you don't miss much, do you? Yeah, okay, if you want to watch one, it's fine with me."

"I'll be through in the kitchen in a few minutes. Go relax, boss."

Denny sat in the living room in his dad's old recliner while he watched CNN on the flat-screen TV. Tim was busy in the kitchen.

While he was relaxing in the living room, and as Tim was finishing up his work in the kitchen, Denny saw Tim's cell phone on the end table. Detective that he was, he did a sneaky thing. He took Tim's cell phone, his own cell phone and a pad and pen into the bathroom and closed the door. He put his phone on vibrator and then took Tim's phone and called his cell phone number. When the call came through, he wrote down Tim's number that had registered on his own phone. He copied down the number and slipped it in his pocket. The number had also been saved in his phone's memory. Then he went back to the living room and replaced Tim's phone where he had found it. Tim was still busy working in the kitchen. Tim already had Denny's number on the phone, so he didn't think he'd realize he'd been snooping.

A few minutes later, still wearing the robe, Tim came into the living room carrying a glass of wine.

"Want a little more wine?"

"No thanks, I overshot the runway already."

"Well, the kitchen is finished. Everything is back in place. Monny will never know. Do you want me to pick out a DVD to watch?"

"Yeah, okay."

Tim looked through the bookcase with its many DVDs.

"What would you like to watch? Any preferences?"

"You pick one out. I'm probably going to fall asleep and have to head for bed in a bit anyway."

Denny had made up his mind. It was best to have Tim stay in the apartment overnight. He couldn't think of a decent alternative.

He said, "I think it's probably best if you stay here for the night. Before you get started with that DVD player, let me show you the guest room where you can bed down."

Denny led Tim down the hall, turned on the lights, and showed him the guest bedroom. It was where his father and mother stayed on their New York trips. Then Denny and Tim headed back to the living room. Tim continued looking through the DVD collection.

"How 'bout *In Bruges* with Colin Farrell? Have you seen it? He's a hot dude. He should shave more often though."

"Yes, but I don't remember it too well. I know I liked it. That's fine with me."

Tim obviously knew his way around DVD machines. He loaded the DVD slot and soon had it up and running on the big flat-screen TV that Denny and Monny had recently bought.

Tim spread out on the couch to watch. Outside they could hear the thunder and see flashes of lightning as the rain continued coming down heavily.

Denny still felt distinctly uncomfortable. It was unusual for him to be sharing the living room with any male other than his father.

After a while Denny had a hard time keeping his eyes open. He'd had a tough day of it.

"Look, Tim, why don't you stay up and watch the film. Just turn off the machine and the living-room lights when you're finished. I've got to hit the sack. I'm exhausted."

"No, you go to bed any time you want. Don't worry about me. Good night, Lieutenant Denny."

"Good night."

Denny went into his bedroom and closed the door. He wasn't worried about Tim rifling through things, and there were no prescription drugs in the bathroom of any use in case he was a druggie. Denny doubted that anyway. Tim certainly wasn't going to take off. He was genuinely terrified of some people out there. He was on the run in a sense.

Denny got ready for bed. He decided not to take an Ambien. He was very tired but didn't want to be "doped up" in case something happened during the night. Denny always slept in his briefs and tee shirt, and he followed his usual practice. He climbed into bed and pulled the comforter up to his neck.

The rain was still coming down fiercely outside with the wind howling and roaring. Denny could barely hear the film playing in the living room. Tim had the sound turned down low.

Twenty minutes after he'd climbed in bed, there was no sound coming from the other room. Apparently Tim had shut off the TV and headed for bed.

Denny had a hard time sleeping in the house when people other than his father and mother were staying the night. It would take him a while to get to sleep. Restless, he kept turning from one side to the other attempting to find a comfortable position.

Some time later, he heard the bedroom door open. He sat up. He saw Tim standing in the doorway in the dim glow coming from the hall night-light. He was still wearing the bathrobe.

There was a break in Tim's voice. It sounded as if he were crying.

"Denny, do you mind if I come in and talk to you for a bit?"

Reluctantly Denny said, "All right, but we've both got to get some sleep. Make it short, okay?"

Tim sat at the edge of the bed. Denny knew for sure Tim was crying.

"Denny, what am I going to do with myself? I don't want to die. How can I get away from these guys?"

"Tim, I can have you placed in protective custody and taken to Washington or wherever. I can get it done, believe me."

"What good is that going to do? I can't live my life in some godforsaken place."

"Tim, we have the resources to protect you."

Tim was sobbing. He seemed to Denny on the verge of a breakdown.

"Denny, please, I need your help."

He had his head in his hands.

Denny thought, *This a human being, just a kid, a desperate kid in a tough spot. You can't let him just sink. Suppose he was my boy? Would I abandon him?*

Denny patted Tim on the back.

Tim put his head on Denny's shoulder. Denny flinched.

"I'm going to die. They're going to kill me."

"No they're not. Get ahold of yourself."

That was always a bromide that never worked. That only exasperated a bad situation, made things worse.

"Hold me, Denny. Please hold me."

Denny tried to comfort him. He held him in a half embrace, but it was a very awkward situation for him. This was not a guy thing at all. Denny felt weird, but he also felt that he owed the kid something.

"I'm so scared. Let me get into bed with you. Please let me stay here for just a little while until I can calm down."

"No, I don't think that would be a good idea at all. I think you should go back into the guest room and try to get some sleep."

Tim was sobbing uncontrollably. Denny held him but not tightly. He tried to do as much as he could to calm him down. For fifteen minutes the sobbing went on. Tim was shaking. Then after a time Tim stood up. The bathrobe fell away, and he climbed unbidden into bed next to Denny under the covers.

Denny was paralyzed. A heterosexual male adrift, not knowing what to say or what to do. A naked guy in bed with him. *Shit!* Wanting to show compassion, but being careful not to let down his guard. Tim was after all a gay man. Their bodies barely touched under the covers.

Tim's body was shaking. He didn't seem able to quiet himself down and stop the trembling. Denny thought, *I've got to get up. Get dressed and sit in the living room. Get myself out of this situation before it goes too far. But he's only a kid. He's me at that age. God, if I wanted or needed a little comfort, wouldn't my dad respond. Would he abandon me?*

Time passed. Tim had moved a little closer and was lying

facing Denny's body, their bodies just barely touching. More time passed. The shaking stopped. After what seemed like a long time, Denny could hear even breathing and soon gentle snoring. Apparently Tim was asleep. More time passed. Denny didn't know when, but at some time he too fell asleep.

When he woke again, it was still dark, and rain was drubbing on the windows. Denny was on his side, and Tim's body was cuddled around his. *Now what do I do?* Denny tried to move out of the embrace. There was a slight move by Tim, and he felt himself pressed closer by Tim's body, now with their bodies squeezed together.

Tim's arm was wrapped around Denny's body. Denny discovered it felt comfortable, comforting to him. It was another human being wrapped tightly to him, bonding, connecting.

Denny realized he had an erection. Momentarily he was frightened. His body was reacting in some instinctive way to this situation that he didn't understand or didn't want to understand.

He could feel a hardness against his backside. Then he felt the kiss almost before he quite understood. Tim's lips had nuzzled him on the back of his neck and lightly kissed him.

Tim gently turned Denny over, and they were face-to-face. Denny quietly acquiesced to this. Tim kissed him on the forehead and then the eyelids.

I should push him away, get out of this bed and get the hell away from him.

But Denny did nothing. Then Tim's lips were on his. Tim kissed him softly, tenderly. Denny barely responded, but he could feel it. There was an acceptance, an instinctive response on his part. Tim kissed him again. Tim's lips were parted, but Denny's were not. Denny could feel Tim's warm tongue. Denny did feel a thrill to it.

I shouldn't do this. I can't do this.

But it was an impulsive reaction. He didn't know why, but he let Tim kiss him and hold him tightly. Tim's hand was exploring. Tim put his hand under the waistband of Denny's briefs and held his penis as he kissed him. For some time Tim kissed Denny's cheeks and lips while still grasping Denny's firm penis.

Tim pulled the covers back. He moved over Denny's body and edged Denny's briefs down. Denny arched his body slightly so that Tim could pull his underwear down and then remove the briefs.

Tim's lips and tongue were on the head of Denny's penis softly licking, his tongue caressing and revolving around the head of it. Then Denny could feel the head of his penis in Tim's warm mouth. Tim gently took Denny's penis into his mouth and then slowly immersed the whole organ in his mouth.

Denny fully felt the sensation. It was extremely pleasurable and satisfying. It was so easy to just give in and feel the pleasure and delight for a time. He just relaxed and surrendered to the feeling. Minutes later Denny could feel that he was reaching climax. Then he came, fully, gloriously. That feeling of a slow death. It felt very fulfilling. It felt good and right to Denny.

Tim moved his body up next to Denny's and held him tightly. Slowly Denny came back from the ecstatic climax to a point of satisfying relaxation.

Later, their bodies still held in an embrace, Denny drifted off to sleep.

When Denny awoke, with sunlight filtering in through the blinds, he was alone in the bed. His briefs were bunched up at the bottom of the bed under the covers. He pulled them on up over his groin. He got up and pulled on his jeans. He looked around the bedroom. The bathrobe lay on the floor. He could smell hot coffee brewing.

He walked to the kitchen. The aroma of coffee came from the Mr. Coffee machine. The door of the bathroom was open. He looked in. There was no sign of Tim's clothes. No sign of Tim anywhere in the apartment. No note, nothing. Tim had disappeared.

Denny didn't want to think about what had happened. He felt no guilt, no shame. He did feel a closeness to Tim, but to

Tim he would never mention what had happened, nor would he ever tell anyone else about it. He poured himself a cup of steaming coffee, walked to the living room and stared out the window. It was a bright sunny day, and down on the street delivery trucks were busy supplying the various restaurants. Puddles remained from the rain, but the street was bathed in sunlight.

Denny felt that no wrong had been done, nothing untoward had happened, just that two human beings had had a brief connection. The river of life flowed on.

35

Two days after Tim's visit to the apartment, Denny got a call from Monny. She was on her way back from her sister's apartment in Mineola and would be home shortly. When she came in the door, he gave her a big welcome-home hug and kiss.

"So how is Sis doing?"

"Still carrying the torch. As usual she blames herself for him taking off. Says it was her fault because she nagged him too much."

"Your sister nagging? Never. She couldn't possibly do that. A little prodding maybe, some noodging, but not nagging."

"Don't get sarcastic. We both know she's got a lot of issues she has to work her way through."

"I know that, hon. Uh, while you were away, we had a visitor here in the house."

He wasn't about to say, *Oh, by the way I had a male hustler here who slept with me overnight and gave me a great blow job.*

"Male or female?" Monny asked.

"Male, a young guy named Tim who's been providing us with information about the river killings."

"Is that the same guy that you ran up to Provincetown to see? Where you had all the fried clams with bellies that you could find?"

"Yes, he's become a source for the serial-killer case. A nice kid."

"Was it a wise idea having the guy here in the house? He's a hustler, isn't he?"

"I couldn't refuse him. He's been followed for the last few weeks by persons unknown. He really believes that he's going to end up a victim. He was terrified. And, yes, I assume that he's a hustler."

"With an entire police force of thousands of officers, couldn't some of them in that vast organization track down the people who are following him? How safe does it make me feel when a whole army of cops is impotent and helpless?"

"It's not as easy as all that to catch them. First of all we don't know where Tim's going to be. He's not a decoy."

"How long did he stay?"

"He stayed overnight because he was scared out of his wits."

"**Overnight? A hustler? Here in our house?** You gotta be kidding. Tell me you're kidding. I thought there was a detail camped outside this house. They didn't see anything? He said he was being followed, and they didn't know it? What good are they?"

"I did check with them. They didn't see anyone. They didn't know anyone was heading for our place until I opened the door."

"He slept here overnight?"

"Yes."

"How old is this Tim?"

"Early twenties. Don't worry, I washed all the sheets and remade the beds."

"Beds? How many beds did the kid sleep in, for Christ sake? What did he do, try out every bed in the apartment? What is he, a mattress tester?"

"Now who's being sarcastic? No, he just slept in the big guest bedroom. I figured as long as I'm washing one set of sheets, I might as well wash them all."

"I don't know. The whole thing sounds awfully fishy to me. He was in the bathroom, right? What about the medicine cabinet? What about the cash in my desk drawer?"

"Oh, Jesus, Monny, I'm enough of a judge of character to know this kid isn't a druggie or a thief. We have no addictive prescriptions in the medicine cabinet. You know that. Unless he stole some Ex-lax. And the cash is intact, believe me."

"If this kid is in such danger, how come he isn't in protective custody?"

"We can't put someone in protective custody unless he gives his permission. We don't have enough to go on to force him into it."

"Is this kid going to be a regular visitor? I don't think I like the idea of my stud muffin having a male hustler here in the house at his beck and call. He could displace me if I'm not careful. It sounds ominous to me."

"Believe me, he'll never be back, and I wouldn't allow him back in."

"Is he gay?"

"I have no idea."

"Wouldn't it be important for you to know that your so-called source is or is not gay?"

"Some hustlers are; some aren't. It's none of my business right now."

"I don't like the idea of some young gay hustler crying wolf and then making moves on my husband."

"I don't think he's faking, and I don't think he'd come on to me."

"Why are you so sure?"

"Look, Monny, I gotta get going. Believe me, this kid won't be allowed back."

"What if he shows up at the door?"

"He won't be back, and if he shows up, don't let him in."

"Is he cute? Would I be turned on by him? Were you?"

"Monny, I gotta go."

"Okay, hon, but remember, if I find a good-looking hunk out on Broadway, I may get the hots for him and bring him back here for a quickie."

"Look, I'm outta here."

He gave Monny a big hug and a kiss and fled out the door so she wouldn't entrap him into saying more than he already had.

As he closed the door, he felt guiltier than he had after Tim's fateful departure.

36

Smitty, the homicide detective manning the phones, greeted Denny when Denny walked into the squad room. Smitty said, "We got a call from a kid who gave only his first name."

Denny asked, "And?"

"Here, listen to the tape."

Smitty turned the recorder on, and a young man's voice spoke, "It's a cop you want for those killings along the riverfront."

Denny recognized Tim's voice. *Oh, shit!*

Smitty's voice could be heard on the tape, "How do you know it's a cop?"

"A cop in his car was hitting on me. Trying to get me to go with him."

"A uniformed officer?"

"No, a guy in regular clothes."

"How do you know he was a cop?"

"What the fuck you think I am? A dummy? I can tell a cop car a mile away. Listen, I've been in touch with Lieutenant Delaney. Please get through to him and tell him I'm in deep shit here. He knows me. Tell him it's Tim. Before it's too late, get Delaney, please."

On the tape Smitty could be heard saying, "I'll get in touch with Lieutenant Delaney right away. Why'd this guy pick on you?"

"'Cause I was working the street."

"Which street?"

"East Fifty-eighth between Second and Third."

"What'd this guy say?"

"The usual shit. I can't remember the words."

"What'd this guy look like?"

Denny's mind was racing. *Oh, my God, what's happening?*

"How the hell do I know? He was in the car. It was dark. I couldn't get a good look at him. The window wasn't all the way down. You cops stick together. Cover up for each other. How do I know you're even going to follow up on this? He didn't get out of the car. Do you guys ever use your legs and feet when you got wheels? Oh, shit, he's coming back. I may end up on a slab in the morgue if I'm not careful. Please get Delaney."

The phone went dead. Denny panicked. He tried Tim's number over and over again but got no answer. He got ahold of Rich and Terry and told them about the phone call, and for the rest of the day and night he continued trying to reach Tim on the phone. Then Tim's phone went dead, and he couldn't get through at all.

37

When Denny got the call at four a.m., he knew it could be very bad news. It was Rich.

"Denny, this time it's on the East River near the Triborough. We just got the holler. It's a young guy laid out like a corpse in a coffin. The usual pattern. This time our perp might have made a mistake. Homicide has got some tire tracks, and there may be a credible witness. An off-duty fireman saw a van turn off onto a dirt track near the river right near where the body was found."

Twenty minutes later Rich picked up Denny, and they headed crosstown toward East River Drive. When they got to the scene, they saw the yellow tape, lights flashing on patrol cars, the floodlights, a forensics team in jumpsuits pouring quick-drying plaster into tire tracks. Denny had a feeling of dread; he felt creepy, had a premonition of something bad about to happen. As he got closer to the laid-out corpse, he couldn't believe his eyes. His body swayed, and he covered his face in his hands.

He moaned, and then cried out, "Oh, Christ, it's Tim. Oh, my God. Oh no, please, not Tim."

Denny tipped his head back and looked up at the heavens. His body rocked back and forth.

Rich stood absolutely still and silent. Minutes passed. Then, Denny turned and went back to their SUV. He opened the rear door and sat in the back seat with his head in his hands. Rich didn't follow him. Denny was the boss. When Terry showed up, Rich cautioned her, and the two waited some distance away.

Finally after some time had passed, Rich approached the vehicle. He knocked on the window. The window rolled down. Denny said, "Give me a couple of minutes. You and Terry know the drill. Get started, and I'll join you. Handle as much as you can. Probe the mouth for a condom, and . . ."

His voice started to break up. The window rolled shut.

After another ten minutes, Denny climbed out of the back of the SUV. He felt like a dead man. Robotically he walked close to the crime scene. He waited another minute and looked down again. Tim looked serene. His pallor was a ghastly white in the bright glow of the lights. His body was laid out reverentially.

Denny spoke very quietly to Terry, "What do we have so far?"

"All the usual. As you can see, the usual arranging of the body, a set piece. One big difference in this one. This time we found two condoms in his mouth. It's as if the killer was thumbing his nose at us. But a possible big breakthrough. This time we have a witness. That tall guy standing over there, a fireman on his way home from work, and a set of tire tracks that the techs are pulling. He was your source, this kid, wasn't he?"

"Yes, I guess you can call him that. I placed him in danger and didn't protect him the way I should have."

Terry did not comment. She was wary of saying more than was necessary, judging from Denny's intense reaction to the discovery of the body.

"Denny, is there anything I can do? Anything you need?"

"About what, Terry, resurrecting the dead? Turning back the clock?"

There was a long pause. Minutes passed.

Then Denny said, "I'm sorry, Terry, don't listen to me. I grew to know the kid, grew fond of him. He didn't hurt anyone, but please forget my personal comments. I'm still here. I'm not gone yet. What I can do for this kid is find the bastard who did it. Let's deal with the case just as we would any other case. The witness. The tire tracks. Our guy is messing up, screwing up, losing it. We're going to get him."

Terry said, "Denny, we're very close to closing in on this bastard. I can feel it. We're almost there."

Denny said, "The witness, he's a fireman? Let's talk to him."

Rich was standing next to the witness. The man was in his early thirties with a ruddy face. He looked exhausted.

"My name is Kenneth Laughlin. I was on my way home from work. I live way out on Long Island, in Patchogue, Suffolk County. About six hours ago I saw this enclosed van really slowing down. I was pissed off. Ready to honk the horn. I was just coming off a real rough twelve-hour shift. Then his signal light goes on, and I see him turn down this dirt road. Something got me suspicious. Why that time of the morning in the dark? I thought of the river and the killings right away. I don't know why. I just did. I called it into Nine-one-one. They sounded very skeptical, but they said they'd check on it. After I got home, the Suffolk cops showed up and rushed me back to this place. All I can say is that it was a white van."

Denny asked, praying at the same time, "Did you happen to get the license number?"

"No, not all of it, but I did get the last three numbers though because it's my birthday. They were six-two-zero, June twentieth."

Terry said, "We've got Motor Vehicles working on it, Den."

Denny said, "Kenny, did you see the driver?"

"No, not at all, but there was a passenger in the front seat, though. A man. I didn't get a look at him either, but there were at least two people in the van."

Denny looked at Terry and Rich, and they were all struck by this new lead.

Denny said, "Tim claimed there were at least two people stalking him. He was right. Why the heck didn't I listen?"

Denny spent a lot of time at the scene, but could not find anything striking.

Finally he said, "Give strict instructions to everyone here that no one is to reveal to anyone there was a witness or about the tire tracks. No one is to know within or without the Department. This is to be kept in a very tight circle. Don't even let The Pigmy know at this point unless he asks you directly."

The three of them went back to their SUV. Rich and Terry sat in the front seats, and Denny sat in the back with his laptop open, the glow of the machine eerily lighting up his stricken face. He started reviewing the extensive river murders file. He was searching for some path that might lead him in a new direction, a different way of looking at the case. God knows, everything else had failed.

He said to the others, "Tim never gave me anything definite, no breakthrough that would lead me to the killer. Except at the end he was convinced that he was being tailed by at least two people."

Denny went back to the computer file. For some reason he brought up the two e-mails sent to Monny. He remembered the psychologist saying that they were probably the work of someone other than the killer. He studied them, read them over and over. Rich and Terry in the front seat were getting impatient, antsy.

Then the word *commonalities* leapt out at him.

On his computer he went to Edit, then to Find. He typed in *commonalities*. The only place he found the word was in the e-mails. It did not appear anywhere in his written reports.

He said, "Guys, do you remember me using the word *commonalities*? That we should be looking for *commonalities* in these homicides."

Rich said, "Yeah, it's a word you used sometimes. I think you used it when we first started this case."

Terry said, "I remember you using, it but vaguely."

Denny said, "Did I ever use it anywhere else in front of anyone you can remember?"

Both answered in the negative.

Terry said, "You might have used it at one of our meetings with The Pigmy, beg pardon, Captain Fazio, but I can't really be sure."

"Damn. I know I used it in talking to someone, but I know now from looking in my computer I never put it in writing. You both take good notes. Go over your notebooks and see if the word appears in your write-up of some meeting, okay?"

Both agreed.

Denny said, "Okay, let's get going. Sorry that kid's death affected me so much. Terry, you have techie friends in NYPD's antiterrorism unit. Could they track down a cell phone number for me?"

"Oh, I'm sure they can."

"Good. Try to get me a list of incoming and outgoing calls and see if you can track down the names of other cell phone numbers that pop up."

Denny gave Tim's cell phone number to Terry.

She said, "Okay. I don't think that'll be too hard for those folks. They're always snooping on everybody. Nothing's off limits these days."

"Let me know if you get anything. It's Tim's cell phone number. That is if he still used that particular phone."

Then Denny had another brainstorm. On his laptop he looked up the e-mail Hal Madden had sent him about the Odd Man Out case. He went through the list of bars. He read it over and over, and then it hit him. The Death Pool. In his call to Stennis, Stennis had said that his hangout was The Flotsam. There it was on Hal's list. A coincidence? He didn't think so. A piece of evidence to tie Stennis in with this whole case. Stennis might have known Tony Angelli, the Odd Man Out, Victim Number Seven, from the bar. Maybe Angelli knew something or maybe he just became another piece of deadwood.

38

Denny's avenging angel instincts, like those Michael Connelly had invested in his series detective Harry Bosch, began to tug on him. The effect that Tim had on him clicked into place. Few killers would ever have the deep and abiding desire for vengeance that began building up in him.

Many things started to gel in Denny's mind, and his intuition was beginning to kick in. He thought of his father's warnings, Tim's pleas for help and his belief that there was more than one person after him. The psychologist's analyses started to come together with other information.

Denny was getting bad vibes out of some of the things he had been hearing about Stennis and Slattery in the Sex Crimes Unit. Something smelled, something wasn't right. It just didn't compute.

He sat down with Rich and Terry, and they went over a lot of worrisome pieces of the case, like pottery shards that had to be reassembled and put together.

Denny said, "Remember the first meeting with Stennis and Slattery? How come Stennis knew so much about hustler bars when he wasn't on the Sex Crimes unit in those early days? Was it just hearsay he got from older cops or was it firsthand stuff from playing around himself in those early days? I'm sure now I used the word *commonalities* at that first meeting. Does something smell fishy here? Were there people other than you two who heard me use that word?"

Terry answered, "I think you used it at our first meeting with The Pigmy. Then I'm pretty sure you used it again at the first meeting with the sex crimes people. Rich, Hal Madden, Marco, Stennis, and Slattery were there."

Rich said, "Oh, Den, I've turned up something interesting. Stennis and Slattery own a business on the side. They have a car rental business. It's not a big operation, but it apparently brings them in some extra income. Madden and Smitty are going to look into it right away."

Denny said, "Okay, Terry, let me know what you find out about Tim's cell phone calls. In the meantime I'm going to begin talking to some people. I'm going to start with Lieutenant Marco. I've got a gut hunch."

An hour later, alone, Denny sat down with Lieutenant Marco.

"Lieutenant, a lot of things have turned up which put your guys, Stennis and Slattery, in the crosshairs. Surely some of this has been leaching back to you. It has to be."

"Yeah, I've been hearing things. Stuff that's really bothering me. If I thought my guys were even peripherally involved, I'd . . ."

"Of course you're very protective of your men. That's only natural. I'd be the same way."

"They're my guys. They're my responsibility."

"But you've always seemed overly defensive to me, as if something didn't ring true to you."

"Hey, Delaney, don't go too far. Why don't you . . ."

"Listen, Lieutenant, we can either talk this out here and now just between us, or we can take my suspicions to the commander level, and then, you know, the shit will really hit the fan."

"Okay, Delaney, this is just between the two of us."

"You have my word. Do you mind if I call you by your first name, Lou? And, please call me Denny."

"Okay, Denny, here goes. I have some things I want to get off my chest. For some time I've felt these two guys are up to something. Not in on the take or anything like that. They are always huddled over their personal laptops. They are too damn close. Too tight. I can't put my finger on it, but to tell you the truth, I've been thinking of breaking up this whole unit and getting a whole new crew. I don't think these guys should have anything to do with sex crimes, especially male sex crimes anymore."

"Why, because you feel they're up to something?"

"Yes, and because they're too wired to this whole thing. Too close for comfort."

"Like rogue shit?"

"Well, yes, in a way."

"What kind of rogue stuff?"

"Hey, if I knew something tangible, I'd tell you. This job has become too much of a desk job for me. I'm inundated with paperwork. It's as if these two are running their own show, their own shop. They were both here before I got this assignment so I was reliant on their expertise. I'm just a robot here. You knew they had a rental car business on the side, didn't you?"

"Yes, just recently we found that out."

"Yeah, they do. They rent out mainly vans. Between them they've got a lot of dough. Over the years they did a lot of smart day-trading. They have a lot more dough than I have. That's for damn sure. Sometimes I just sit here and watch them running the show. I think the reason they never took exam promotions was that it would crimp their style. They're too satisfied with things the way they are."

"Which is?"

"Denny, I honestly don't know, believe me, I've even told my wife that I feel like a fifth wheel in this unit. They're up to something. What it is, I don't know."

"Could one or both of them be responsible for these homicides?"

"Oh, God, no. That's beyond imagining, but I've heard scuttlebutt that says your team is looking at them. I've been thinking of going to Internal Affairs with all this crap, what you're up to, and what they might be up to. It's ruining my sleep at night, believe me."

"Have you faced them, asked them directly about this?"

"How do you go up to your own men and accuse them of something so terrible?"

"Lou, are we agreed we're now allies in this investigation, or are you going to continue to obstruct?"

"Yeah, Denny, I need your help."

"And I need your help. First I've got to see your duty rosters for all the nights in question. Do these guys ever patrol the areas in separate vehicles, or do they always team up?"

"No, sometimes they do individual patrolling. Not always on the same nights. One might be off on a particular night, and the other one's on duty."

"So how much oversight do you have over them?"

"Very little. It's only very recently that I've become very uncomfortable with them operating almost like independent contractors."

"Please get me their individual roster assignments as quick as you can. Now let me ask you some things. You knew all the details of the case, the investigation as it was developing. You were kept informed?"

"Yeah, pretty much."

"You knew about the careful, respectful arrangement of the bodies, the condoms found in the mouths of the victims, the fact that I found an address book on one of the victims, the mocking e-mails that were sent to my wife."

"Yes, I knew all that. I read the files, and I kept in close touch with Captain Fazio. We're good friends. We go way back together."

"I bet you do. The two of you. That would figure."

Marco said, "Of course. I know you don't like what I do, and, for that matter, you don't like me. But I had to keep myself up-to-date on what you and your squad was doing because it affected me and my men, even though you don't like it."

"What about *commonalities*?"

"You mean elements of the case that are in common, like correlations."

"No, I mean just *commonalities* as a word."

"I don't get it."

"Remember the first meeting that I had with you and Stennis, Slattery, Hal Madden, Rich, and Terry?"

"Yes, of course."

"I used the word *commonalities*."

"So what?"

"You used the word *commonalities* in your threatening e-mails to my wife."

Marco's reaction was immediate. He turned red and looked like a guilty child.

Marco said, "Are you nuts? What the hell are you talking about?"

"I know that the killer didn't send those e-mails. An expert source has told me that this serial killer leaving condom talismans would have no reason to advertise in such a blatant way. He would have everything to lose and nothing to gain from sending those e-mails.

"You included the word *commonalities* in the nasty messages you sent to my wife, dragging her into danger and also spreading some harmful Departmental scuttlebutt about Terry and me."

"Delaney, have you gone out of your fucking mind? You've gone completely insane. Do you realize how far you've strayed from reality?"

"We now have the proof that you're the one who sent the e-mails. Do you also want to go down as the serial killer as part of an overall charge or is the e-mail charge a loner?"

Denny was bluffing, but at this point he had nothing to lose.

"You used the word *commonalities* in your reports."

"No, Lieutenant, three people have checked, and I did not. I am going to hang you out to dry for what you did to me and my wife."

An angry Denny stood and hovered over the man he knew was guilty. He could see it in Marco's eyes and face.

"You scum, you're going to lose everything for what you did with those e-mails. If you want to face homicide counts along with your asshole buddies, let me know now."

Marco stared down at the desk. He loosened his tight collar and started taking deep breaths.

Denny said, "Decide now which crimes you're going to admit to. Your chances of facing first-degree murder charges are very high. Or are you going to admit to sending those destructive e-mails? Make up your mind now. You have very little time."

Marco's upper body collapsed, and he slumped over his desk. He started to weep.

"Decide, you fuck! Right now!"

"Denny, I'm sorry."

"Sorry doesn't do a thing, you asshole!"

Denny turned and opened the door, ushering in two men and a woman from Internal Affairs. He turned and saw a defeated and deflated Marco throw his badge onto his desk.

Outside the building Terry and Rich were waiting for Denny in their vehicle.

Denny said, "Why did he ever have to send those e-mails to Monny in the first place? Christ, talk about a lousy world full of creeps. Now I'm going after Stennis. Terry, please, drop word to him that he can find me outside of Katya's."

39

At the time Denny was starting his meeting with Lieutenant Marco, a beat-up old Crown Victoria and three police vans were pulling up outside the Adams Car Rental Agency in Corona, Queens. Hal Madden and Desmond Smithwick, known by one and all as Smitty, detectives in Central Homicide, marched up to the small cinderblock building in the back of a fairly large parking lot where rows of vans and cars were arrayed. From the newly arrived vans on the street, six men and women in jumpsuits, all members of NYPD's forensics department, emerged and started assembling their gear, readying to get the okay from the two detectives.

Madden and Smitty entered the small office and walked up to the counter. Behind the counter sat a heavyset, florid-faced middle-aged man who was munching on a hero sandwich.

"What can I do for you gentlemen today?"

He set his sandwich down, wiped his mouth with a napkin and slowly drifted to the counter. The two detectives showed their ID wallets to the man.

Hal said, "Hi, I'm Detective Madden, and this is Detective Smithwick. And to whom are we speaking? Are you Mr. Adams?"

"No, I'm Lester Sinclair, manager of the company. Old man Adams has been gone for ten years now. I think you'll find him in Tampa, Florida. That's if he's still aboveground. I think he had a bum ticker."

"We're not really looking for him. You're the guy we want to talk to. These papers I'm presenting to you are court orders which give us the right to search the premises, all vehicles on the lot and impound anything that might aid us in our investigation."

Lester examined the documents and then looked up.

Madden said, "If it's not too much trouble, we'd like you to give us a rundown on the business, how it operates, ownership, etcetera, etcetera."

Lester said, "I imagine that you gentlemen are familiar with the fact that the business is owned by two of your compatriots, two members of the New York Police Department."

"And their names just for the record?"

"Detectives Harley Stennis and Jerry Slattery. About ten years ago they bought the business from Adams and kept the name because businesses beginning with A are apt to be the first ones people see in the phone book, and the first numbers they call."

"Yeah, gotcha."

"Perhaps you informed Officers Stennis and Slattery before you made this raid?"

"Lester, this isn't a raid. It's a lawful search with a court order. Big difference. And it doesn't matter whether the king and queen of England are the owners of the business. The fact that they are policemen is immaterial to this search."

"I think I better inform Stennis and Slattery about this anyway. Or their attorney."

"Lester, I'm going to ask you to hold off on any phone calls for a while. Otherwise we might have to report that the manager was uncooperative and was impeding a lawful search. Just hold your horses awhile. I wouldn't want to charge you with obstruction or of being an accessory to a serious felony when it wasn't necessary. And you wouldn't want to go before the judge who issued these orders. She's a stickler, and when somebody contravenes one of her court orders, she gets very testy. She's old-school. Guaranteed Her Honor would certainly slap you with jail time for being in contempt. Smitty, signal the crew, would you please?"

Smitty went to the door and gave a thumbs-up, and the lab workers fanned out over the lot. They started checking the tire treads on all the vans. One tech was in and out of the office matching keys on a board with the vehicles in the lot.

Hal said, "Les, let's get down to business here. How many

vehicles in total does this company own or lease or handle?"

"We have eight passenger cars and nine vans. They are all owned by the rental company. We deal almost one hundred percent with companies, businesses. We don't really have a retail trade. We provide loaners to repair shops for vehicles being fixed. We get very little tourist trade."

"How many vehicles are off the lot right now?"

"Three vans and two cars. Business has been very slack lately. The recession has hit us hard. Luckily the owners aren't reliant on the business for their basic income. I'm lucky they're absentee owners with good jobs."

"Les, in the last eight months have you sold or traded in or gotten rid of any of your vehicles?"

"No sir."

"What hours are you here in the office?"

"Strictly eight to five, Monday through Saturday. A six-day week, but I'm happy to have it. And I get to see my wife and kids plenty on that schedule. Any more time at home, and I'd drive my wife berserk. And the kids are happy, two late-teens, who have lives of their own. I never come in here early or leave late. The bosses want it that way, and that's the way I like it."

Smitty asked, "Are you ever here at night?"

"Never. It's strictly a day job."

"Do Sergeants Stennis and Slattery ever come in at night?" asked Madden.

"Oh, yeah. They're in and out of here all different hours."

"How do you know?"

"Oh, the way things are moved around. Sometimes a vehicle is moved. Sometimes they leave the computer on. Papers will be rearranged. They're here all right. Quite often."

"Do they ever use one of the vehicles?"

"Oh, sure, from what they told me years ago, they have a deal with the NYPD where the cops use some of the vehicles for surveillance and undercover work."

"Do you have the paperwork on that?"

"Oh no. They handle that whole end of it. Hush-hush stuff. It's all done through them."

"Do you see payment for this Departmental usage in your books?"

"No, they take care of all of that. I imagine your police accounting department could fill you in on police invoices and such."

"Les, in other words, you're saying that you've been told that the NYPD is using your vans or cars for undercover work?"

"Yes, that's the way I understand it. Hey, it might even be part of this new terrorism push by the cops. You know, Homeland Security backup, all that kind of shit."

"Could be. Lester, have you had occasion to change tires on any of the vans or cars in the last few months?"

"No, not that I know of. Charlie's garage across the street handles all our maintenance including some of the cleaning of the vehicles, and I have his invoices on that stuff. We haven't needed tire changes in months. I told you business is slow."

"Would Stennis or Slattery change a tire?"

"No, I doubt it very much. They would leave a note that such and such vehicle needs a tire change, has a flat, etcetera, and I'd have one of Charlie's boys take care of it for us. You know our business has been way down. Drastically. What the hell is all this about? Are Stennis and Slattery on the fiddle or something?"

"Lester, we'll tell you what you need to know. We're doing just fine so far. Let's keep it that way so we don't have to drag you into court. That judge can be a real bitch."

Smitty looked out the window. Forensics was everywhere in the yard. In addition to tire treads, they were checking inside the vehicles.

Madden said, "Les, we want the tag numbers, registration number, plates of every vehicle the company owns or has access to. Could you do that as a personal favor to me?"

Lester gave Madden the fish eye, thinking that Madden was being a wise guy, but he didn't want to cross him. He was a mean-looking bastard who appeared something like a jowly basset hound. A lot like Jerry Orbach on *Law and Order*. Better not to cross him.

"Yeah, I got all that on the computer." He went over to the computer, looked at various screens, and then found the one he wanted. Soon the printer underneath the counter could be heard running. Lester handed a list to Madden who quickly looked at the list to see if any tag numbers ended in 620. None did.

Madden said, "Did anyone here ever switch plates for any reason? Did you ever use a dealer's plate?"

"No, we always kept the correct plates on the vehicles. It's funny that you should say that because Charlie, our repair guy across the street, was grousing to me about some license switching at his place. One morning he came in, and a car that didn't have plates the day before had the plates of the car next to it the next morning, and the other car was missing plates. He was really pissed because he figured maybe some kids were doing some joy riding."

Madden said, "We'll talk to your friend Charlie when we get through here."

"You know, Detective, I'm just an employee here. How do I know how much I'm supposed to give you?"

"Lester, my boy, we have the right to take you and everything in this office down to police headquarters. You're doing just fine. Les, is there one or more particular vehicles that your bosses use?"

"I wouldn't know. I'm not here when they take them out. I'm just a cog in a machine here. I never got the feeling they were up to anything."

"Are there any other employees?"

"We have a part-timer who cleans and washes the cars, gets them gassed up, takes them in for grease jobs. Works two days a week. I know for a fact he's legal. We have an old lady, a bookkeeper who used to work for Adams. She comes in one morning a week."

One of the techies came in and motioned to Madden, who went outside with him.

The techie said very matter-of-factly, "Behind the building there's a big pile of old tires to be recycled. Using our blow-up photos of the treads from the site of the homicide, we've found a definite match. It's a sure thing. Believe me, it'll hold up in court."

Madden called Smitty out and told him.

Smitty said, "In this job some days you get lucky."

Madden called Denny on his cell phone and notified him of the find.

Denny said, "Great, Hal. I'm about to pay a visit to our friend Stennis. I think things are beginning to gel at last. When you wrap things up there, let Rich and Terry know."

40

Denny was standing outside Katya's on East Fifty-third when Stennis pulled over to the curb in a black Mercury. He was by himself. The passenger window rolled down, and Denny leaned in.

"How she hanging, Denny? What's up? Why're you casing this gay hangout?"

"Oh, I don't know, Harley, maybe something's been bugging me, and I just have to check out some details."

"Isn't that our job? To do the leg work for you guys?"

"I've been starting to feel funny about this whole case."

"Why, what's up, Champ?"

"I don't know, Stennis. Something smells fishy to me. I grew up around cops. Cops were my best friends since I wore diapers. With my dad I used to spend a lot of time in precinct stations. There was something about certain cop shops you could smell a mile off. Cop shops always smelled different from other places anyway. The smell of too many guys being in a place too long, sweat, the smell of fear, maybe it was adrenaline. Like rotten crap sometimes. As if some feces had stayed too long in the colon. Rotted longer than usual, longer than in an ordinary civilian's colon."

"Kind of graphic stuff you're talking, my friend. Meaning . . . ? Maybe it's pure crap that's bugging you."

"Yeah, crap. No such thing as pure crap. Fetid, long-lasting rotten-to-the-core cop shit."

"Denny, are you trying to tell me something? Are you trying to get to me, or am I just imagining here? Are you trying to get me pissed off? I been a cop longer than you've been on this planet."

"So, you want a medal, Sergeant? Maybe you've been a cop too long."

"Just clearing the air, Lieutenant."

"No, why would I want to get a fellow officer of the law pissed off? Why?"

"Denny, you haven't got your hand on your piece, have you?"

"Maybe I do. I have a reputation for being too quick on the draw. I'd appreciate it if you'd keep your hands where I can see them."

"My piece is still holstered, Den. Why are you doing this? What's your beef with me?"

"May I open your door and get in?"

"Sure, why not? You're a lieutenant. I'm a lowly sergeant. Also you could blow my head off if I don't."

"Okay, I'm about to open your door."

"What is this, a fuckin' screenplay? Are you taping this shit? Are you wearing a wire, for Christ sake?"

"Just keep your hands on the wheel."

"Oh, jeez, what the fuck's going on here?"

"I said just keep your hands on the wheel where I can see them."

"And if I don't?"

"I really will blow your head off."

"And your story will be what? You shot a fellow officer because you thought, *thought*, he was reaching for a gun? Have you gone nuts, Denny?"

"I need to have some serious questions answered."

Denny opened the door and settled into the passenger seat. He was very cautious, watching Stennis. He saw that the car was not in gear so Stennis would have to put it in gear to move it. Denny had his hands on the grip of his gun, and Stennis had his hands on the steering wheel.

Denny said, "We usually talk of opportunity and motive in any investigation, right?"

"Of course."

"Let's talk about familiarity with the victims."

"Yeah, sure, anything you wish, Lieutenant."

"You knew the victims."

"Uh-uh. A few of them I knew by sight, but I never saw

some of the others. I certainly didn't know them."

"What if I have a wit who says you knew several of the dead boys, enough to talk to, enough to have them in your car?"

"I'd say you got some bullshit liar trying to save himself from some charge."

"I've got a couple of wits who say you're gay. Is that something you've ever admitted to anyone? Wouldn't it be important for the Department to know that one of their guys dealing with male sex crimes was gay? Not that that would disqualify you. In my eyes it would make you more of an asset."

"I'm not gay, and anybody who accuses me of it is a pure bullshitter, got it? You know you're doing everything here but accusing me of being a killer. What the fuck is this all about?"

"Oh, I don't know. I think it's about a cop who doesn't know right from wrong."

"Who the hell are you talking about?"

Dennis eased his weapon into his hand.

"Whoa, man, what the hell has gone wrong with you? Have you gone ape-shit or what?"

"Listen, Stennis, I have a theory."

"Wow, listen to this. A college-educated cop with a theory, all the while with his piece in his hand."

"No, a streetwise cop with an instinct for not only a rotten apple on the force but an evil bastard. Don't give me any of those college-educated digs, because I'd love to blow your head off right here and now. Reach for your piece, and I really can make it look like self-defense on my part."

"Yeah, like you did with Felix the Cat, not once, but twice. Are you nuts? Have you lost it?"

"No, I'm onto your shit. You and your buddy Slattery have gone off the reservation and become killers."

"Listen, Delaney, you better hear what I have to say, because I have alibis for those homicide drops."

"How do you know you have alibis? Only a guilty man

would know in advance to have a ready excuse like that, make such a statement."

"Hey, I'm way ahead of you. Days ago I could tell the way you and your sidekicks were sniffing around asking questions that you suspected me of something. I knew you'd be looking around for a scapegoat because you have no suspects. So you blame the messenger, or anyone in sight. You'd try to nail anyone for your incompetence.

"By the way, Delaney, how come one of the victims, Tim O'Neill, spent the night with you at your apartment? What was that all about, huh? Getting a little male nookie on the side? Looks to me like you ought to be on the suspect list. Maybe you're the one who should be outed, the guy who may be the closeted gay. How 'bout that, Rambo? I'm not the only one who knows about that little dalliance, you know."

This threw Denny way off-stride. *How did he know? What did he know?*

"What the fuck are you talking about, Stennis?"

"Got your alibis for the nights of the drops, wise guy? Going queer on us? Are you a closet case?"

"Stennis, I think you'd better back off when you're sitting in a car with a guy with a weapon who has enough to hang your ass."

"Delaney, you know you're never going to make any of this stick. You've got no case against me."

"We've got enough to hang you, you scumbag, I wish you'd reach for your piece so I could splatter your brains all over your windshield.

"You're an insane fuck, you know that?"

"We're pulling you in."

Suddenly Stennis flew open his door and jumped from the car, yelling "Shoot, Denny, while you have a chance. Make me a martyr, you fuck!"

Denny reached out to grab him, but he wasn't worried about Stennis getting very far.

Outside the car were Terry, Rich, and three other detectives, all with drawn guns. Two uniformed officers had shotguns pointed at Stennis.

Terry yelled, "Stennis, freeze. Don't even try to do anything or go anywhere. If you do, you're a dead man."

Stennis looked around him. A car blocked the street ahead of him and another covered the intersection. If he ran, he knew he was a goner.

Slowly he raised his hands above his head. Denny was out of the car behind him. He quickly frisked Stennis and disarmed him. He shoved Stennis's arms down behind his back and cuffed them. He read him his Miranda rights.

Quickly Stennis was hustled into the back of one of the unmarked cars. Sirens started screaming, and a caravan of cars took off down the street.

Within minutes he was booked in Central Homicide. Captain Fazio stood there watching. Very little was said. Stennis was put in a cell.

Denny took off with Rich and Terry, and they rushed to Slattery's house in Queens where they would hook up with other detectives who had been dispatched there earlier.

41

Slattery lived in Floral Park on Long Island. The house was a modest colonial built before World War II on a fifty-foot-wide plot. Aluminum siding had been added at a later date. When Denny, Rich, and Terry drove up in front of the house, there were already two unmarked detective cars on either side of the street, and a SWAT team van sat at the corner.

Denny said, "I'm going in by myself. I'll let you know if I need help."

He walked up to the door and rang the bell. Within a few seconds, the door was opened by an attractive brunette in her early forties. She looked like someone's wholesome mom from a 1960s television sitcom. She had a weak smile.

She asked, "Lieutenant Delaney?"

"Yes, ma'am."

"My husband has been expecting you. My name is Irene. Is there anything wrong? Any trouble?"

"No, Irene. I just have to talk to your husband about some police business. Everything is going to be all right."

"I hope so. He's been very worried and agitated lately. I have to take off and pick up our two boys. They're staying with my folks out in Smithtown. Jerry told me to take off as soon as you got here, but I'll stay around if he needs me. He's in the basement in his workshop. He told me to show you the way and get going."

Denny followed her into the kitchen. She opened the door to the basement and yelled down.

"Jerry, Lieutenant Delaney is here. I'm sending him down. I'm going to get going, pick up the kids, and I'll be back in a couple of hours."

From down below Denny could hear Slattery yelling up to his wife.

"Yeah, Irene, just send the lieutenant down here, and I'll see you later. You get going, honey. Love you lots, Babes."

"Me too, Jerry. I'll be back soon. Bye-bye."

"Thanks, hon. Bye, now."

"Lieutenant, do you want me to go down with you, show you the way down?"

"No, I can find my way just fine. You just get on your way, Irene."

"Bottom of the stairs, his workshop is over to the left. Okay, nice meeting you. Sorry I'm in such a hurry, but you must know how it is with kids."

She turned and headed for the back door. There was a light on at the top of the stairs. When he got to the basement, the only light was to the left, a large overhanging shop light over a wide wooden workbench. Jerry was seated on a high stool behind the workbench facing Denny, and another stool was in front of the bench. It was an ominous setting with the only bright light coming from beneath the metal hood of the shop light. Slattery was bent over some work and didn't look up until Denny got closer.

"Sit down, Denny. You don't mind if I call you Denny, do you?"

"Of course not."

"And it's not going to bother you if I put some finishing touches on this model?"

"No, not at all, Jerry."

Slattery had the contents of a do-it-yourself kit laid out in front of him. He was building a World War II model aircraft carrier. There were tools, a pot of glue, and some small kit pieces spread out. To the left on the workbench was a cell phone and an army-issue 45, the grip close to Jerry's hand. Slattery saw Denny staring at the gun.

"Don't worry about that. I was just cleaning and oiling it. You have nothing to fear, believe me. I wouldn't hurt you for the world. Besides, I know you didn't come here alone. I just got word that you nailed Marco for those e-mails. That was a damn stupid move. A dumb thing for even a cluck like him to do. What the hell did he think he was accomplishing?"

"I have no idea. Jerry, would you mind if I turned on my tape recorder?

"No, be my guest. I also heard that you've locked up my partner, Stennis."

"Yes, he's in custody. Boy, you have fast and reliable sources."

Denny turned on the recorder. His mind was racing. Could he possibly grab that 45? The gun was at the edge of the work table very close to Slattery's hand. He knew that he had to get information out of Slattery. That was essential.

"And, Denny, don't bother reading me my rights. That won't be necessary. I want to clear the deck here and get as much as I can off my chest."

Slattery was working on the flight deck of the model carrier. He looked up, and the blue eyes were as hypnotic as ever.

"Denny, I have a story to tell you. It began right here in this neighborhood. I grew up in this house. It belonged to my parents who now live in Arizona. This was my dad's workshop. We worked together building models just the way I do now with my own sons.

"My wife Irene grew up in a house across the street. We've known each other since before kindergarten. We were childhood sweethearts, soul mates really. There was never another girl for me. We went through school together, always boyfriend and girlfriend, dating. I love her more than any other woman on earth. We got married when we turned twenty-one. Neither family objected because to them it was a foregone conclusion."

"She's very beautiful."

"You bet she is. Yes, she's a stunner. Always has been. In high school we were king and queen of the prom. Ours was like a storybook romance. A love made in heaven.

"Now, Harley Stennis and I have worked out a true account for all this, and we did it weeks ago. We knew you'd be on our trail eventually. But, please let me tell you my story before you ask too many questions."

"No, you go ahead, and tell it in your own way, at your own pace."

"And don't insult my intelligence by telling me that Harley made a full confession and implicated me. That's not the way we planned this whole thing out. We agreed that he wouldn't say a thing until I did."

Slattery paused and wiped his forehead with his handkerchief. He wasn't sweating, and it wasn't an overheated basement. Denny thought he probably wanted time to put his thoughts in order.

"When I was fifteen, I met Stennis in the local Y. At that time it was a guys-only place, and all the men and boys went swimming in the nude in the Y pool. Dicks swinging, you know the scene. A big pool in the basement of the building. It's kind of creepy telling you this after what I told you about Irene, but it's the truth.

"I was always turned onto older guys. Like guys in their thirties and forties, not real old wrinkled men. When I met him, Stennis was in his mid-thirties. Always had a good body, worked out, took good care of himself. Sexually I was turned onto him when I saw him in the shower room and walking around the pool area in the buff. That was just me, the way I am.

"He was outgoing, friendly. Extroverted. You know how he is, gabby. Took an interest in me. We liked each other. It flattered me that an older guy would be interested in me. A fifteen-year-old punk kid. At first I didn't realize it was sexual even though, as I say, I was attracted to him. Don't ask me why. I realize now I was bisexual. Yes, it does exist. I'm living proof of it. I loved Irene with all my heart, but maybe it was such a convenient love for me, what with the two of us growing up together, that it wasn't such a stretch for me to love a man and a woman at the same time. I was a boy in love with a girl, but I wasn't in love with another boy, I was in love with a real man.

"Simultaneously with my love for Irene, I had desires for

this older guy. I dreamt about him. Maybe I should say mature, because I certainly wasn't into old men. I guess it was being bi. In my mind, I could balance my love for Irene and my desire for Stennis. I'd go to the Y when I knew he'd be there. And later I found out he was doing the same thing. Two horny guys, I suppose.

"Stennis and I would be in the shower together, and I'd get a semihard-on watching him soap up, and he got hard too. Something about his looks, his body, something drew me to him. And we were both voyeurs.

"Upstairs in the Y we'd play pool or table tennis, and in the gym we'd play pick-up basketball. Then we started going out for burgers together. A movie or two. I told him all about Irene, and he was very supportive. I really connected with him, and he liked the idea I had a girlfriend. Maybe it made me straight in his eyes. Being straight is very important to him. I never told my family that I had an older friend. They would have cottoned onto something.

"Then one day he brought me to his apartment. I knew he was a cop, a detective, and I admired him for that. There was no booze, no pot. We took a shower together. He didn't seduce me, but we ended up in bed together, and for me it was like my whole life suddenly made sense. It was real. I fell in love with him, and he fell in love with me, and to this day we're still in love. And I still love Irene too. It's as simple as that. He never became possessive, so it was never Harley versus Irene. He let me be my own person, and we got together when it didn't interfere with my dating Irene. Irene never knew him until much later, and she never knew we were lovers."

Tears were coursing down Slattery's cheeks though he was still talking. Denny knew enough not to interrupt.

He went on, his voice breaking only slightly, "I'm not a psychologist, so don't expect me to explain human psychology and behavior. I know what I am. As I was getting older, Harley and I got together often, and he taught me almost everything I knew about sex. I was a virgin with women, and

Irene and I didn't have sex until about six months before we got married.

"Then one day I told Harley I wanted to marry Irene. He was great. He was very much in favor of the idea. He knew that I loved her, and that I wanted kids, a family. He just hoped that the two of us could be together sexually after the marriage, and he promised not to do anything that would interfere with the marriage.

"Irene and I got married. Stennis was at the wedding. He wasn't best man. I wasn't that cynical. From that moment on, he became good friends with Irene. I'm sure that she never suspected anything was going on, even though Harley and I continued fooling around, well, having sex, as we had before.

"As time went on, Harley talked me into joining the Department. It had been in my mind ever since I met him. I don't want you to get the idea I was Harley's trade. No, we were full-fledged lovers. I wasn't a lay-back, believe me. Don't knock it until you've tried it, I always say to myself."

Denny flinched a little at this statement.

Slattery continued. He was no longer tearing up. "After a few years Harley got himself assigned to Sex Crimes, and later I was able to get on the squad so we started working together.

"Unfortunately, tragically, as it is in a lot of gay relationships, we started to seek out variety. Men are pigs. Most of them are by nature promiscuous, I think. Well, Harley had always liked a bit on the side, and he occasionally went with hustlers. He never liked outright gays, flaming queens or queeny guys. The straighter-acting, the better. That time in the office when he was describing johns to you and your squad, inwardly I knew that he was generalizing and basically describing himself.

"Well, as I say, Harley had some flings. He didn't talk about them, but I knew. One time I went to his apartment. We never had sex here in this house. I compartmentalized my sex life. Anyway, I went to his place, and he had a hustler there. One thing led to another, and we ended up in a threesome. We had threesomes only a couple of times. Harley and I still enjoyed sex with each other, and I still loved having sex with Irene. As time went on, very rarely, I would pick up a hustler on my own and go to a motel with the trick. That was my downfall.

"Denny, see that refrigerator over there in the corner? Would you like a Bud or a Diet Coke? I'm getting thirsty and wouldn't mind a nice cold Bud."

"Okay, I'll have a Coke."

"Would you go over there and get yourself a can of Coke and bring me back a Bud. I've got a church key here to open it."

Denny dutifully went over to the refrigerator to get the drinks. He realized he was being sent so Slattery could keep his eye on the 45. The refrigerator had lots of beer and soda and also a bottle of vodka and a container of orange juice. Denny brought the drinks back to the worktable. Jerry opened his beer and took a big swallow.

"Tastes good. Hits the spot. As I was saying, when I went out with a couple of hustlers, that was my downfall. One time I was in Houston on my own to attend a workshop. I had a rented car. I picked up a hustler and brought him back to the hotel. To make a long story short, I contracted HIV/AIDS, and I gave it to Irene. I didn't know all this until long after. I was tested at one of those anonymous places, and found out I was positive. I told Harvey, and we were very careful having sex together after that. Also after that I never had sex with Irene without using protection. I never told her I was positive.

"I know it was that kid in Houston because I didn't see anyone after him. Irene was in an automobile accident, and she was injured. Not badly, but enough to require that she have a blood transfusion. Months later she was at her doctor's, and they just happened to give her a full battery of tests. She turned out positive for HIV/AIDS. She blamed the transfusion, but I know I gave it to her before I tested positive. I went nuts. Completely round the bend, lost it. Harley saved me.

"I had been seeing a doctor secretly and getting the full antiviral treatment. I never told Irene anything about my HIV. When Irene found out she had the virus, they put her on the same regimen, but with her own doctor.

"I knew and Harley knew where she picked up the infection. Harley and I talked about it for weeks and weeks. We both worked it over, chewed on it, gnawed on it, sought someone to blame. Harley blamed hustlers from the start. Of course I blamed myself for what had happened to Irene, but the two of us kept working it up in our minds. It became an obsession. We couldn't drop it. We became paranoid. Maybe there's such a thing as joint paranoia.

"Someone had to pay. And then it became, 'They have to pay. They have to be punished.' It was like a disease with us. I know we both flipped. From that point on our minds were twisted. Don't ask me to explain. I don't know why. Hour after hour, day after day, we plotted. It was stupid. It was insane.

"I really believe that both of us by reinforcing each other made it happen. We talked each other into a complete state of nuttiness."

Slattery took another long swig of beer. Denny was sipping his soda, staring at the man who at times continued working on his model ship, seldom looking up at Denny who thought he was watching a warped mind imploding.

"The condom in the mouth was my idea. The arranging of the bodies was Stennis's doing."

Denny instantly realized that Slattery had made a huge leap forward into his narrative. He had left out the initial killing, and perhaps the real crux of his insanity.

Slattery continued, "Stennis and I, as you no doubt know, own a car-rental agency. We rent cars and commercial vans. We'd usually use one of the vans to pick up a kid. A few times we picked up a kid in a Department vehicle. Don't ask me who did the actual strangling. We took turns. It was sick. I know that, but my love for Irene and my love for Harley clouded my judgment. What these kids were doing to ordinary people, how could it go on? Someone had to pay. We couldn't let that continue, could we?

"Stennis and I knew the working boys, and we decided they had to be stopped. If we killed a few, the rest would be scared off, head for cover, even disappear. They were infecting innocents. I know I'm mad, off my rocker, absolutely bonkers, but because we were sure of ourselves and our mission, we lost all reason. Don't think I didn't pray. But once we got started it was so easy, and you and the whole Department were so fuckin' stupid and incompetent. We even delivered one of the bodies in Stennis's boat, and no one in the Department even figured that out.

"In only a few cases we targeted particular kids. We knew Tim was a conduit to you, that he was talking. At the end we started following him. We weren't worried when you and your team were assigned to the cases, because we knew that you knew squat about working homicide cases. We were worried about Madden because he'd been working homicide for years. You earned your reputation chasing a terrorist. What you knew about working homicide cases could be put in a thimble, even though you got some FBI training at Quantico."

The dig pissed off Denny, but he let it go. It didn't mean anything. More important to understand the warped mind of this guy.

Slattery said, "Okay, any questions before I go on?"

"No, no, Jerry, please just go on with your story. But when you guys used to go out with hustlers, didn't it become known on the street that you two were fooling around?"

"We didn't go with that many kids, but kids come and go, and I don't think the ones we did go with knew we were cops. And they disappeared from the scene long ago."

"Whose idea was it to start killing these kids?"

"It was the both of us. We did everything together. Right after we killed a kid, Stennis and I would have good sex. No, great sex, better than ever. If that isn't sick, I don't know what is. I still love Harley, and I always will."

Denny was angered by Slattery's calm explanation of the

homicides. He saw a hammer on the workbench and thought how great it would be to grab it and slam it down on Slattery's hand closest to the 45, and then go from there and beat his head into a pulp. He was sitting there calmly listening to the maniac who had killed Tim and all the others. But he knew his best course was to get as much information out of him as possible. Would the guy try to make a run for it? Denny had heard other vehicles pulling up outside. If Slattery nailed him, he knew that if he ran for it he'd face a fuselage of gunfire outside.

Denny said, "Why didn't the two of you just walk away? You were both eligible for retirement and good pensions. Both of you could have retired. You and your wife were on the drug regimen. You could both live for decades. Why the fuck was it necessary for the two of you to execute, punish innocent guys for your indiscretions? Two selfish pricks, deluding yourselves with your mission, to punish the world to satisfy your fucking sick love affair."

Now Slattery was angry. His hand inched closer to the 45 as he said, "Are you trying to get me pissed off with your moral judgments? Why the hell should I care what you think? How the hell do we know what went on between you and Tim in your apartment that night? Maybe you swing both ways too. We knew you and Tim spent the night together, Mr. Fucking Moral Judge.

"But don't think you're going to piss me off and get me to do something stupid before I get a chance to tell my full story. I know I would be taken out by a SWAT team that you have waiting outside. I'm not that much of a jerk.

"I told Harley that I would make a full confession, and we'd both take the consequences. He'll do the same. Don't think I'm going to be sappy enough to take a shot at you. I admire some things about you. You're basically an honest straight-shooting guy who believes in a just world, the same way I do."

Denny winced inwardly but asked, "What's Harley going to do?"

"He's going to validate everything I say, and we'll both go to the chair for what we believe."

"And what does he believe?"

"He believes in the strength of our love for each other."

"Why were the victims laid out so reverentially?"

"Because they deserved the rites of the dead. The dead deserve our respect. To us these hustlers were worse than parasites, lower than scum, but once dead, they had to be honored, had to be respected as human beings who'd gone astray."

Denny thought about the expression "naughty but nice" the psychologist had used, and the two sick minds they had become, reinforcing each other. What annoyed him was the way this guy seemed so calm and rational as if he had decided to tent his house for termites instead of deciding to slaughter kids.

Denny said, "What about the living? Don't all living human beings deserve the chance to live? Who appointed you and Harley as judges, jury, and executioners?"

"And, Delaney, who appointed you judge, jury, and executioner for Felix the Cat, eh?"

Denny had to deflect him so he said, "And what about the condoms, Jerry?"

"That was my warning that unprotected sex is a serious crime, one deserving condemnation. Punishable by death."

Denny grimaced a little at his last comment.

"Jerry, you remember the case we called Odd Man Out, that didn't fit the profile of the others. Our lab guys found carpet fibers from a vehicle that matched with one of the hustler victims, and both fibers matched ones in one of your rental vans. That guy wasn't a hustler. Why did he have to die?"

"Stennis did that one on his own. He's going to tell you the same thing, so I'm not being a snitch here. I didn't know about it until later. Harley thought it would throw you off-stride and confuse the issue. If I'd known, I'd never have agreed to it, but Harley said it was necessary. Now I know that I got so deeply into this swamp that there was no way back. God cannot forgive what I've done. Tim was to be our last one, and then it would stop and be over. It can never be over for me. There is no way out for me."

What a sicko, thought Denny while he said, "Jerry, can we walk out of here now together so you can give yourself up? Make it easier on your loving wife and children. Why make them suffer? They love you. Don't you owe that to Irene?"

"No, Denny, I can't do that."

"Why not?"

"Because my life would be all over the tabloids. Do you think I could face Irene and the kids for what I've done. Isn't it weird that I know that? I was hoping that I could go for this gun, and you'd draw your piece and shoot me, execute me the way you did Felix the Cat, not once but twice."

"No, Jerry, I'm not going to do that. I guess you're just going to have to kill me and take your chances."

"Uh-uh, Denny, I'm not going to shoot you. You've never been the enemy."

"Jerry, please, your death won't solve . . ."

With unbelievable speed, Slattery picked up his weapon and placed the barrel to his lips.

"Please, Jerry, don't do that. You'll never be executed. You know the appeal process. The years of delay. The way executions have been put on hold in New York for decades. You and Stennis can get good lawyers, and you can plead insanity. Think of Irene and your boys. You'll always be able to see them. You'll never be executed, you know that."

"I destroyed Irene and my family a long time ago by what I did. I've gone past the point of no return. What we did is beyond horrible. There is no excuse on earth for what we did. God cannot forgive me. I can no longer stand to live with myself."

In the close quarters of the basement, the blast was deafening. Denny couldn't hear after the discharge. His ears were ringing. The bloody mess in front of him sickened him, and he slid to the basement floor.

About a minute later the SWAT team set off a charge at the front door. The door popped open, and a team of heavily armed, armor-vested men rushed through the house. Denny had risen, pulled the lanyard holding his badge and ID outside his shirt where the officers could see it. He raised his hands over his head and stood at the foot of the stairs. When the team came through the door, he yelled, "Police. Everything is over."

Deafened, he couldn't hear a thing they said, but just stood there with hands above his head. The team quickly secured the area, and Rich and Terry led him up the stairs. Outside he pointed to his ears and said, "Can't hear."

He stood outside on the door stoop, resting on a railing. Minutes passed. Gradually his hearing returned. Terry and Rich waited with him. Denny noticed that his shirt was covered with blood splatters.

After he had given them a complete account of Slattery's confession he said, "Slattery, boastfully, and gloating over it, said that they had delivered one of the bodies in a boat owned by Stennis. I want you guys to do everything you can to find out where this boat is kept. When you find out, have forensic teams go over it with everything they've got. I'll bet Stennis cleaned it thoroughly, but we may get something from this that will nail him with concrete evidence in case he doesn't prove to be as forthcoming as Slattery was."

Terry said, "You don't think Stennis is going to talk and tell us everything after his lover's suicide?"

"I think that Stennis's survival instincts are going to come to the fore, and we're going to find him clamming up. Let's nail him with evidence we find at the boat and in the rental fleet, the tire treads, the carpet fibers."

When they returned to the station, they brought Stennis into an interview room. Denny told him what had happened, and Stennis was devastated. He rested his head on his crossed arms and wept. Denny waited. Minutes passed. Then Stennis spoke.

"I'll have nothing to say, and I want a lawyer."

Denny said, "Do you wish to make any kind of statement at all?"

"Nothing. Just let me get in touch with my lawyer. Jerry's death is all your fault, Delaney. Don't expect me to help you recoup your losses. You're going down in flames, hotshot."

Denny said, "I should have blown your fucking head off in the car when I had a chance."

Denny left him there living with his delusions.

42

Tim's parents were in their forties, pleasant people, both good-looking, easy to get along with. On the phone they had asked Denny if they could meet with him, and he quickly assented. He had borrowed Fazio's office, a comfortable room that didn't have an institutional look to it. The couple sat on the leather couch while he sat opposite them in an armchair. They had agreed to coffee so Denny had brought in cups for them.

Tim's mother said, "When he was seventeen, he told us he was gay. We weren't to tell anyone else, and he only told his best friend about it. None of his other schoolmates. He said, 'I don't want to be a martyr, and I'm not on a crusade. Hell, I know what kids are like.' He had a very happy life in high school, played lacrosse, was on the gymnastics team, had great parts in the school plays and was very popular."

The father continued. It was probably something the two of them had worked out together. "When Tim first came to New York, he wanted to get into acting. He started at drama school, and he was in several of their productions. Somehow he met an older guy, a man in his sixties, a very cultured, cultivated man. On a trip to the city, we met him. His name was Roy. Very nice guy. He took a great shine to Tim, and Tim moved in with him. Tim began taking an interest in art, in opera, in cooking, in a lot of things because of Roy. They were together about a year.

"Unfortunately Roy had a massive stroke and heart attack and only lived about a few weeks beyond it. Tim was devastated. It was really the first time he had faced a death of someone very close to him. Roy's relatives came to town, and Tim was thrown out on the street. Roy had left him a legacy of ten thousand dollars, which was very good of him. Tim moved in with some friends from drama school, and he worked at several good restaurants to keep himself going."

The mother was brushing away tears, but she was able to go on. "We were shocked when we found out Tim had been murdered by two policemen. We know that you're probably protective of your own kind, but I still think it's horrible for two police officers to be guilty of such ghastly things. He was our son, and he deserved better out of life. What kind of a world is this?"

The mother and father were both teary-eyed. They were holding hands. Denny wished he could offer some words of comfort, but he wanted them to talk and let out their feelings. God knows he was feeling very sad about the whole situation.

Now the father began again, "Then after his death we learned that he had been hustling. We never knew. He had called us a couple of times a week. Everything was going well, he said. Life was good. We heard about you, and we know you're a good man. But bent priests, sick cops, people in authority, why can't they have the decency to get out of their positions and face the real world where they don't have power over people?"

Denny said, "God, I wish I knew. Tim was a great person. I can't excuse those two maniacs, but I just want you to know that I grew to like your son very much."

The father said, "Thank you for caring, Lieutenant."

Tim's mother said, "We're not going to pretend we knew what he was up to in the city. He did say he had met a famous detective. He named you, and in our last talk he even said he had developed a crush on you. We knew he trusted you. We think he loved you, and that you seemed genuinely fond of him even though, as he said, you couldn't reciprocate his love."

Denny said, "If I had known him better, I'm sure I would have loved him like a brother. But like a big brother my biggest regret is that I couldn't have protected him."

When they stood to leave, Denny, eyes full of tears, hugged each one in turn. He went down to the street with them where they all said their goodbyes. After they had gone, he just wanted to go to a bar and drink himself into a stupor, but he knew that wouldn't solve anything.

43

Denny and Monny were seated in the Rum House bar, the small space off the Edison Hotel lobby. A performer friend of theirs named Paul had just finished singing at the piano bar. He had given a beautiful and moving interpretation of "Time Heals Everything" from Jerry Herman's Broadway musical *Mack and Mabel*.

After applauding Paul, they turned back to their conversation. Denny had told her everything about Slattery's confession and Marco's role in the case. Monny wanted to know why a police lieutenant had written the two nasty e-mails, and Denny had no real answer to give her.

"Why would those two policemen sworn to uphold the law go on a murder rampage? That still doesn't make sense to me. Maybe I'm dense when it comes to the minds of psychopaths."

Denny said, "I think the two of them flipped, went off a cliff together. Reinforced each other's insanity. I can't really explain it. If I try to make sense of it, it doesn't compute. Two sick minds. Wickedness and evil of that order can't be figured out. Monny, I may have to leave the Department. I can't figure out anything anymore. Idealism only goes so far. Two rotten apples here, another one there.

"How can I go on when it's my own organization that is sprouting these evil bastards? Maybe I'd be better off working in the private sector. Perhaps I should give up police work and spend time figuring out how these sickos develop. Perhaps work with psychologists like Doc Estermass trying to figure out what makes these people tick and flip."

Monny said, "Denny, don't get to be a cynic and a loser. What drew me to you in the first place was your sense of mission, that the good guys had to be there to stop the bad guys. Part of your magnetism was your belief in the infinite possibilities of accomplishing good things. Don't go back on me now. Keep at it. There will always be rotten apples in every walk of life. Look what I deal with on a day-by-day basis in the financial world. What those creeps do on a daily basis.

"No, Denny, you're much better at reacting to what's happening, and going from there. You do well when you're being a cop. I feel safer when you're on the beat. At heart you're a flatfoot like your dad."

"Give me a break, hon. I just have to do a lot of thinking. I'm just feeling my way along. I think tomorrow I'll probably go back to thinking that police work suits my temperament."

Monny gave him a kiss and a hug that reignited his love for her and made him realize how important she was to him.

"Monny, what do I do with a guy like Stennis who refuses to confirm his partner-lover's confession, words said just before his lover blew his brains out?"

"Den, did you ever think that this Stennis was a sneaky bastard, a predator to begin with? I'm going by what you told me about this sicko. A thirty-something brings a fifteen-year-old kid up to his apartment, a teenager who is unsure of his sexuality, and then this older man strips and takes a shower with the kid, swinging his dick, enticing the kid. What do you expect the kid to do? What would you have done at that age?"

Denny felt embarrassed and somewhat guilty.

"I frankly don't know what I would have done at that age."

"But what do you expect the kid to do? He wants to get his rocks off, and here he's being enticed by an older guy. Sure, he could have been bisexual to begin with, but doesn't the blame fall on the older male, an adult, and a cop at that? It was a seduction pure and simple."

"Sometimes, Monny, I think I tell you too much about my cases, but you're right, it was clearly a case of Stennis seducing an underage kid for his own gratification."

"I think Stennis is just staying in character when he doesn't confess. He has been a user all along. But I think it's a good thing you share your cases with me because I see them with a different perspective. I sift through the evidence and come up with the nitty-gritty."

"Thank you for your insights, Inspector."

"You'd think a guy who'd spent a night with a hustler would be sharper about sexual matters."

"Monny, don't start."

Later that night, the two were sitting in their living room relaxing.

Denny said, "Let's have a glass of wine and watch a DVD."

"Great. How 'bout a merlot?"

"That would hit the spot. Got any of that Häagen-Dazs mango ice cream left?"

"Sure, Tiger. Which DVD would you like to watch?"

"How 'bout *In Bruges*? I've never seen that flick all the way through."

"Great idea. With that hottie, Colin Farrell. Oh, listen, it's beginning to rain. Denny, the stars are in alignment tonight."

The rain came pelting down, the windows in the old brownstone rattled, and the wind howled down the Forty-sixth Street canyon that ran from the Hudson River to the East River.

Previous Book by John F. Rooney

Clawed Back from the Dead

In this fast-moving novel John F. Rooney has brought back his series detective Denny Delaney from *Nine Lives Too Many* for a chill and thrill, manic roller coaster ride. A serial killer is on the loose, and he is trying to shut down the making of the movie *Nine Lives, Two Men* that is based upon Denny's match-up with the arch-terrorist Felix the Cat.

Everyone related in any way to the movie is a target in the line of fire. This suspense thriller careens and caroms as it follows a mad assassin. Be prepared to be enthralled with action aplenty as the killer hits his murderous stride. If Denny didn't know better, and if he hadn't killed the evil monster himself, he would think that Felix the Cat was the perpetrator again rampaging, creating havoc and chaos.

Rooney has pulled out all the stops on this one as a murderer conducts a personal vendetta against his perceived enemies in the film industry. The killer seems to be in a race against time as he creates his swath of death. Yet even amid this grim narrative, Rooney is able to inject humor and create memorable characters whose humanity is endearing to readers.

This book helps to round out the portrait of Denny as we see him interacting with his family: his wife Monny, his father, a retired and admired cop, and his brave mother who is standing beside her husband as he battles cancer.

Get ready for a big surprise!

Previous Book by John F. Rooney

The Daemon in Our Dreams

Three strangers in different parts of the world each has three nightmares in which a young Indian man stares menacingly at them. The dreams invoke funeral pyres, glaring skulls and feral beasts. On a land and sea tour from Singapore to the Taj Mahal these three people, Dr. Lee Ably, Fran Carr, and Paul Rowan, separately begin to see the threatening dream daemon in real life, in real time. They have given him a name—Ramesh—but cannot find a reason for his pursuit of them. And how does he get from place to place to materialize before them?

The suspense builds as one after the other of the three travelers is confronted by Ramesh in exotic places. They watch in horror as their daemon changes and evolves in successive sightings into a more deadly foe.

When the trip nears its end, the three think they have found surcease in England, but an Indian hijra message causes them to think otherwise.

In a London hotel lounge three assassinations take place. The assassin appears to be the dream daemon. Why has all of this happened? What ties these three people and their ghostly interloper to one another?

We are drawn into this eerie and insightful story as the book's narrative drive propels and impels readers deeper into the labyrinth. It's an unforgettable tale of human beings facing ominous futures.

Previous Book by John F. Rooney

Nine Lives Too Many

This is a violent and unsettling novel about terrorists, a cautionary tale, but also the deeply moving personal story of a conflicted police detective.

Felix the Cat, only nominally Muslim, but fanatically anti-American and anti-Israeli, is terrorizing New York City and Washington, D.C., with a series of bombings. This third-rate screenwriter plants a deadly bomb which kills and maims hundreds in the Main Concourse of Grand Central Station. The FBI seems in suspicious haste to label it a suicide bombing.

Grand Central Station is Detective Sergeant Denny Delaney's turf. Minutes before the attack Denny has been suspended because his drinking is interfering with his duties. His wife Monny has left him. After Denny barely misses getting killed in the bombing, he examines the terminal's surveillance tapes with his wheelchair-bound, attractive coworker Terry, and he and she realize that this is not the work of a suicide bomber. The bomber has walked away unscathed. After Nine-Eleven Denny had been on TDY with the FBI, and he has made a connection to that duty and the bomber. By threatening to reveal what he knows, Denny gets reinstated to FBI duty so he can work the case.

The novel cascades through a series of suspenseful actions: FBI raids, firefights, ambushes, and attempts on the lives of investigators. Felix, the failed screenwriter, sets up a cinematic conflict between antagonist and protagonist by telephoning Denny. They begin a series of cat-and-mouse, insightful colloquies as Felix's deadly acts of violence proliferate, one for each of his nine lives.

After the Grand Central devastation, nowhere and no one is safe including the streets of New York, the Broadway theater district, the White House, cruise ships, hotels, beaches, and bridges.

Denny has to battle Felix and his alcoholism. Will he be able to win in his inner and outer struggles and defeat a terrorist monster?

Previous Book by John F. Rooney

The Rice Queen Spy

Philip Croft, a master spy for Her Majesty's secret service, MI6, was cruelly outed and tortured for his homosexuality. All his adult life he was a dedicated rice queen—partial only to Asian men. In his life he had three lovers and a few brief encounters. He was a gentle man and a gentleman, a member of private clubs, a man of privilege, who was betrayed by some of his friends—not for being gay, but for being too decent and naïve.

This novel traces Philip's life and his loves, and is a triumphant testimony to a gay man's passage from mid-life to old age. Brushes with death and derring-do followed him even into his elder years. He was able to keep his dignity and live a full life while briefly thumbing his nose at his former superiors by opening a gay sauna in London. Being a rice queen was his preference, but living a fulfilled life was his destiny.

Readers of the author's suspense novel *The Daemon in Our Dreams* will recall that Paul Rowan visited Philip Croft in his London home and told him about his eerie encounters with the dream-daemon Ramesh. In the later pages of this book we see Paul Rowan's fate through the perspective of Philip and his lover Robin.

This book breathes life into a gay man who served his country through deception, and though his country punished him for his personal deception, he became the victor rather than the victim.